P9-CMZ-496

WITHDRAWN
No longer the property of the
Boston Public Library.
Sale of this material benefits the Library.

# PRAISE FOR *THE WOMAN IN THE PARK*

"*Like a Rubik's cube,* The Woman in the Park *twists the perception of reality and fantasy, keeping the reader hooked and curiously searching for the solution. Intriguing, intelligent and multifaceted.*"
**VERA NÄSSTRÖM, AUTHOR & PLAYWRIGHT, *ALL IS AS IT SHOULD BE***

"*Fast and thrilling, Sorkin and Holmqvist's novel* The Woman in the Park *kept me guessing until the final page. There's no tranquility to this Manhattan's Upper East Side, just darkness, disquiet, and suspense.*"
**JAMES STURZ, AUTHOR, *SASSO***

"*This richly textured, beautifully written, and intricately plotted thriller, with a deeply sympathetic female protagonist, is at once a page-turner, a story of loss and redemption, and a beautiful testament to the power of the human spirit.* The Woman in the Park *is a remarkable achievement. I loved it.*"
**CAROLINE NASTRO, DIRECTOR & AUTHOR, *THE BEAR WHO COULDN'T SLEEP***

# THE

# WOMAN

## IN THE

# PARK

### Teresa Sorkin and Tullan Holmqvist

BEAUFORT
BOOKS

Library of Congress Cataloging-in-Publication Data
Names: Sorkin, Teresa, author. | Holmqvist, Tullan, author.
Title: The woman in the park / Teresa Sorkin and Tullan Holmqvist.
Description: First edition. | New York, NY : Beaufort Books, [2019]
Identifiers: LCCN 2019011815 | ISBN 9780825308994 (hardcover : alk. paper)
Subjects: | GSAFD: Suspense fiction.
Classification: LCC PS3619.O756 W66 2019 | DDC 813/.6--dc23
LC record available at https://lccn.loc.gov/2019011815

Émile Zola. (2006). *Thérèse Raquin*. Translator: Edward Vizetelly. Urbana, Illinois: Project Gutenberg. Retrieved March 4, 2019, from www.gutenberg.org/ebooks/6626.

Robert Frost. (2006). *Mountain Interval*. Urbana, Illinois: Project Gutenberg. Retrieved March 4, 2019, from www.gutenberg.org/ebooks/29345.

For inquiries about volume orders, please contact:
Beaufort Books
27 West 20th Street, Suite 1102
New York, NY 10011
sales@beaufortbooks.com

Published in the United States by Beaufort Books
www.beaufortbooks.com

Distributed by Midpoint Trade Books,
a division of Independent Publishers Group
www.midpointtrade.com
www.ipgbook.com

Printed in the United States of America
Cover Design by Michael Short
Interior design by Mark Karis

# MONDAY, NOVEMBER 12, 2018

When the doorbell rang, neither of them reacted right away.

It rang so rarely that at first Sarah dismissed it as noise from a neighboring apartment and took another sip of her bitter coffee, waiting for her mind to fully awaken. Her husband went on reading the paper beside her, barely looking up. His placid face seemed to challenge her sense of purpose, and again she had the strangest sense that none of it had actually happened.

The bell rang again. Eric finally looked up from his paper, his eyes quizzical.

"Are you expecting someone?" he asked.

"No," she said, a slight tremor passing through her. Quickly she got up to answer the door, then paused. Surely Lawrence would not come here, ring the bell for her…No, he'd never do something so careless, not even after leaving her hanging for the last few days. After all, she'd told him Eric was going to be home.

"Who is it?" she asked, not expecting an answer.

"NYPD."

The voice was crisp, official. It took her a minute to register what it had said. Then it spoke again.

"Please open the door, ma'am. We just have a few questions we would like to ask you."

She looked through the peephole. Two men were standing there, neither of whom she recognized, nor were they in uniform.

Panic flared up in Sarah's mind. She looked down at her robe, abruptly realizing she was naked underneath. She tied the belt of her robe tightly, smoothed down her hair with her hands and opened the door.

"Good morning, ma'am," said the older of the two men. They each held up a badge. She noticed the younger one had not ironed his shirt. "I'm Detective Duke; this is Detective Schmidt. Are you Sarah Rock?"

"I'm sorry, is something wrong?" she asked. Fear ran through her as her hands shook. "Oh my God—the kids?"

Eric appeared next to her, equally alarmed. "What's happened?" he asked.

"No, it's nothing like that at all," the older officer said in a conciliatory tone, holding up his hands. "I'm sorry to startle you. We're looking for Sarah Rock—we just have a few questions. Is that you, ma'am?"

"That's me, yes." She pulled the robe even tighter around herself, her heart pounding.

"Thanks, Mrs. Rock. We're looking into a missing persons case and wanted to see if you could help us out with any details." The younger detective, who hadn't yet spoken, was now taking notes in a little spiral-bound pad. "Do you mind if we step inside?"

"Of course not. Come in." She opened the door wider for them to pass through, the words "missing persons" rebounding chillingly in her ears. She'd waited for Lawrence every day this week; were they going to ask her about him?

As they walked by, Eric turned to her.

"Sarah, what's this about?" he whispered.

"I don't know," she said, her voice faint.

The detectives looked at her as they stepped into the kitchen.

"We're very sorry to interrupt your breakfast, Mrs. Rock," the older one said.

"Can I offer you anything?"

The officer smiled, his face businesslike but friendly. "A cup of that coffee would be nice, actually. Just black."

She poured out two cups, utterly bewildered.

"Thank you." The older detective sipped the coffee patiently while the younger drew something out of his notepad and handed it across to her.

It was a photo of a woman. The woman in the park.

"Do you know this woman, Mrs. Rock?" the younger cop asked, his voice surprisingly deep.

Sarah looked again. It was the young mother from the park, the one she'd seen several times before. The one she'd thought looked like a younger version of herself.

She swallowed hard, the blood pounding in her ears. Why were they here talking to her? Had they seen her in the park, waiting for Lawrence?

"Sarah—?" Eric asked dubiously.

She avoided his gaze, concentrating on the picture. For an instant, she imagined admitting that she'd watched the woman in the park before. She remembered vaguely the woman confronting her but wasn't sure what it was about. Her thoughts were jumbled as she pictured herself scrambling for an explanation like a hunted woman, trying to cover for herself as they barraged her with more and more questions.

"Well, what do you think?" Detective Schmidt asked again.

"I don't—" she began, but the words stuck in her throat and she shook her head instead. How could she tell them anything without revealing herself to Eric? How could she—how could any honest person—account for her actions over the past weeks? And where was Lawrence?

The phrase she'd seen inscribed on his ring flashed through her mind, sinister now in its implications. Was this somehow about him? In some way, hidden to her, those engraved words, her fate—and that of the woman in the park—were intertwined.

*Amor vincit omnia.* Love conquers all.

# PART ONE

# ABSTRACT

*Existing in thought or idea*

# CHAPTER 1

# FOUR WEEKS BEFORE

*She kept all the impetuosity of her nature carefully concealed within her. She possessed supreme composure, and an apparent tranquility that masked terrible transports.*
ÉMILE ZOLA, *THÉRÈSE RAQUIN*

A piercing scream cut through the night.

Ripped from her sleep, Sarah sat up, gasping for air. Her heart was pounding in her chest and her breathing was fast and hot. Where was she? She scanned the darkness, searching for clues. She had no idea. Her silk nightgown clung to her body, and the sheets felt moist with sweat.

As Sarah's eyes adjusted to the faint light coming in through the window, the room returned to her and she knew where she was. Home. Her home. 1122 Park Avenue in Manhattan. She felt a flood of relief. That dream. Again. Then came the realization that the neighbors—no, the whole building—must have heard her scream. Her heart contracted in shame.

She looked over to find her husband's sleeping shape beside her. Eric usually awoke to the slightest noise, but no—there he was, breathing peacefully beside her. It must have been a silent scream she'd uttered, a silent nightmare she'd endured. It was the worst kind of nightmare, in a way: the kind that tortured only her.

Silently, Sarah slipped out of bed and out of her nightgown, letting it drop to the floor. She tiptoed to the window and opened it. Dawn was on the horizon; the New York sky dark and heavy. A sudden gust of wind blew in, scattering grains of soil from her plants onto the Persian carpet. She needed air, despite her shivering; she couldn't wait to get out of the apartment.

A shadow fluttered across the window in the building across from hers, and she felt observed, vulnerable. She looked down and remembered she was naked. Her cheeks flared hot, and she quickly stepped back from the window.

She snuck into the bathroom and stood for a while in darkness, letting the dream's last reverberations still within her. That dream—the dark figure hovering over the woman; her and him together, embracing, grabbing at each other. And then there was the sound of a gunshot or something like it. She knew exactly who they were. Eric and Juliette. Images of them haunted Sarah ever since she had found pictures of Juliette on Eric's phone. When she had confronted him about it, he had brushed it off and had said that she had sent them by mistake. Of course she didn't believe him, but she had no real proof.

In the dream, Sarah was always just a spectator to them, fear rising in every part of her body until her scream inevitably woke her up. It was uncontrollable, irrational; the simple fear of having absolutely nowhere to go. How could she do this, time and again—fall asleep and wake up in the same place, and yet never know where she was? How could she feel lost, trapped in her own home?

She flicked on the light and found herself in the mirror. Her blonde hair was ruffled; tired eyes looked back at her. Wrinkles were forming there, defiant of the creams and oils with which she tried to keep them at bay. She touched her face, almost unsure she was real. The creases deepened under her thumb. She knew that others saw her differently than she saw herself. She had been told she was magnetic, youthful, that she was living "the good life." At times she still believed it. She took a deep breath and shook her head.

She opened the medicine cabinet and took out her morning pills. Prozac, 20mg. Two in the morning, daily. She thought a moment, then took one. Shutting the mirrored door, she washed the pill down with a swallow of water and looked at her weary gaze.

It was the dream that made her feel so unlike herself. It frightened her beyond reason to be made to feel so powerless, to wake up confused in a cold sweat. In the daylight she was different; there were good reasons, rationales, behind the things she felt.

She looked back at herself, at the body she still tried hard to keep firm with exercise after two children and fifteen years of marriage. Was that really the problem? No, she could hide those changes under her clothes. Her eyes were the real difference, those seas of blue sadness with nothing to hide behind.

A shadow passed the doorway behind her, startling her. She watched as Eric appeared in the mirror, adjusting his tie. How long had she been standing here?

"You scared me," she said, turning to kiss him.

"What, didn't expect me?" he teased.

"You never know," she said in a tone of mock accusation. In spite of herself she felt ashamed. Had he seen her looking over her own imperfections? Could he have noticed that she'd been going through his clothes the night before? But he only smiled at her, that same smile that had broken down her defenses all those years ago. It still had the same effect on her.

"Come on," he said, kissing her again. "Early start for both of us today."

She watched him as he retreated back into the shadowed room, brushing his teeth. He was dressed already, put together as always; so tall, and strong, and male. *His* wrinkles seemed to show character; the creases around his mouth and blue-grey eyes were beautiful on him, comforting. Sarah now found his salt-and-pepper hair as appealing as she had the dark-brown hair he'd once worn longer. She had always loved him so much—maybe too much. As much as she ached for him, it was worse when he was away—and he was away so often nowadays.

"Kids'll be back this evening," she said lightly, reaching for her own toothbrush.

"Mmm," he answered. "It'll be nice to be together. Remember to call Jason's coach today, by the way."

"Of course," she said. Didn't he know it was already on her to-do list? "What do you have going on today?" she asked lightly. Eric walked past the doorway again, pretending not to hear her.

"I'll wait outside," she heard him say. His voice sounded short; was it annoyance or concern? Sarah could never tell anymore. The more she knew him, the less she felt she knew him. Surely it wasn't suspicion, anyway; she remembered how careful she'd been to put everything back the way she'd found it, the tailored suits and impeccably rolled ties all lined up like soldiers, so he wouldn't notice that she'd been snooping for any telltale signs of Juliette's bright red lipstick on any of his collars. She found herself searching for proof of his infidelity more and more frequently.

Sarah brushed her teeth, pulled her hair into a tight pony-tail—so tight it hurt—and hurriedly threw on some makeup. She emerged into the bedroom. Eric was already gone, in a hurry, as always. Crossing to the closet she slipped into a form-fitting designer dress and high heels. Eric had always liked the heels, the way they elongated her already long, lean legs. Would he notice them today?

"Sarah? Coming?" he called. How could he be gone so often, yet still always be waiting for her?

She grabbed her coat and bag and met him at the door. He took her hand, and she felt the warmth of it entwined with hers. That, at least, felt right. They walked out together through the marble lobby of their building, passing pumpkins lined up cozily in the window. She felt a pang of sadness that there would be no searching for the perfect Halloween costumes with the kids this year. They were going to spend Halloween away for the first time, at boarding school.

"Good morning," the doorman said, holding the door open for them.

"Good morning, Manuel," Sarah answered as she looked at him. "Thanks."

"Of course, Mrs. Rock." The doorman lowered his voice, along with his eyes. She frowned; it seemed even he was looking at her with pity these days. "It's gonna rain out there today," he said quickly. "I feel it. You okay, you got an umbrella?" He offered her one from the vase by the door.

"Thank you," she said.

"Anytime, Mrs. Rock. You have a good one."

"You too, Manuel."

She and Eric stepped out together into the brisk, autumn air. Their building spread out behind them, its formidable Gothic exterior presiding over Park Avenue. It was one of the first high-rises built on the Upper East Side in 1909, and Sarah had immediately fallen in love with its antiquated feel when they'd moved in fifteen years ago. She relished the sculpted animals and dragons crawling up the side, the two large gargoyles at the top; they made her feel part of something old and important. It had taken some convincing to pry Eric away from his dream of a "cool loft space downtown," but in the end they had both been glad she'd persisted. She just wished it didn't feel quite so empty these days.

"Why does Manuel do that?" she asked Eric once they were out of earshot.

"Do what?"

"Treat me like I'm a fragile bird or something."

"He's just being friendly. It's his job."

"I didn't see him offering *you* an umbrella!"

Eric chuckled. "Maybe he has a crush on you."

"Oh please," she softened.

As they walked together down Park Avenue, rays of sun peeked through the clouds. The light glinted off a shiny car, and she caught her own figure reflected back at her, dark and alone. She could already feel Eric pulling away, and she leaned in toward him instinctively. He smiled back at her, and the sky seemed to brighten even more. They stopped at a corner, and without saying a word, he wrapped her in a warm embrace. For just a moment, there was a perfect peace between them.

"I love you," he said, holding her close.

"I love you, too," she answered, and meant it.

"I have to run."

She looked into his eyes. "Me too," she sighed. "You know how she gets when I'm late."

"I do," he laughed, drawing back. "I'll see you later on, okay?"

His gaze accompanied her as she turned and walked a few steps down the block. When she looked back, his eyes met hers and he waved. Their little routine—one of the few that had survived the years. It always made her feel safe to know he was there, watching her go.

She reached the opposite corner and turned back to look for him one last time. He was already gone.

\* \* \*

Sarah looked at her phone and kicked herself. She wasn't in danger of being late for her appointment with Dr. Robin; she'd set the appointment back this week. Now she had an hour to kill. Not quite worth going back home at this point; if she did that, she might not feel like coming back out. Even after almost two years, the appointments were still as difficult as they were necessary. She didn't like to admit it, but she knew she was benefiting from them.

Sarah walked over to Fifth Avenue and entered Central Park. A gust of wind blew around her, waving her coat open and scattering leaves along the pavement. Fall was well underway.

Near the entrance, she stopped to look at a gingko, now naked. A sea of fan-shaped leaves littered the ground under its trunk; the tree had shed all of its leaves overnight. Was it a coordinated surrender? A skill developed over time, to aid it in its famous resistance? It was one of the most ancient trees on Earth, one of the only types to survive the atomic bombing at Hiroshima. She marveled at its seasonal self-destruction, its control over its own desolation.

She walked past the kids' favorite playground and found her usual bench across from it, under the oak tree. She liked to come here to read and be outside; the quaint playground was large enough to lose herself in. She noticed a young mom playing with a little boy inside the playground. The woman was in her late 20's with long, beach-wavy, blond hair, which reminded Sarah of a surfer. Sarah was sure she had gotten sand in her tresses when playing with her son in the sandbox. She remembered those days fondly, and she felt a slight pang of jealousy as she had once also had so much hope, so much engagement with her life. The kids had needed her; Eric had needed her. Life had been so busy, so *full*. She'd taken it for granted that it would always feel that way. And now—

Sarah realized the woman was staring back at her. Embarrassed, she averted her gaze and sat down on the bench, setting her bag beside her, and wrapped herself tightly in her coat. She missed her kids now that they had recently started boarding school; the longing made her heart ache and her mind spin with unused energy. But they were coming back today. She had that to look forward to.

She reached into her bag. She always made sure to have a book with her, and that morning she had plucked one at random from her bookshelf on the way out: *Thérèse Raquin* by Émile Zola. She couldn't remember when she'd bought it, or why; she'd definitely never read it before. She looked at the back cover. Paris, late 1800s. *Better than here.*

She got a pen out of her bag, opened the book and began to read. She chewed the pen, pausing here and there to make a mark in the margin. Zola's words took over and filled her mind; soon she barely heard the kids in the playground shrieking, the little toddlers fighting in the sandbox, the nannies chatting. She was lost in the world of the novel, in the dark streets of Paris, far off.

A stroller bumped her as it rushed past, breaking her concentration. Startled, she glanced up at the young mom from before. Sarah nodded at her but the mom seemed upset. She was yelling into her phone at someone, completely ignoring her golden-haired toddler as he cried over a skinned knee. Sarah felt badly for the little boy and had the urge to sweep him into her arms. The woman glared at Sarah as if she wanted to say something. Stunned, Sarah looked away and went back to her book.

The sun's warmth reached her, and she relaxed into the bench and continued reading. The story engrossed her fully, so she did not realize how much time had passed since she had first settled into the bench. It seemed like minutes, but when she looked at her phone she realized that she had been in the park for an hour. Where did the time go? Abruptly, the air went cold as a shadow loomed over her.

She looked up with a start. There was a man standing in front of her, smiling warmly. He was dressed casually in a plaid shirt, gray jacket, and jeans. He was attractive, she thought at once—actually remarkably handsome.

"*Thérèse Raquin*," he said, his voice dark, deep, and friendly. "Zola. A great writer, flawed in many ways, but good."

Sarah looked up at the stranger. He was tall, at least 6′2″. His face was calming somehow familiar. Did she know him? Surely she'd never seen him before; she would have remembered.

"I'm sorry?" she said.

"I recognized the cover of your book. I have the same copy. Zola was so ahead of his time. All that passion, just pent up. Did you know that his wife had an illegitimate child? And *he* had an affair with his seamstress."

"No, I can't say that I knew that." Sarah's mouth felt very dry.

"Do you mind if I sit?" He pointed at the bench next to her.

"I was actually just leaving." The words spilled out of her and she closed the book, reaching for her bag. He backed up a step, his face conciliatory.

"Sorry, you must think I'm crazy just coming up to you like this," he said. "It's just, I love Zola, and not many people read the classics anymore. I'm Lawrence," he said, stretching out his hand. The wide, warm smile spread further across his face.

Sarah took his hand. She felt a tingle shoot through her arm when he squeezed her hand, his palm was warm and rough. He was even more handsome up close, with deep, blue eyes—*a stormy ocean*, she thought. She couldn't remember the last time she'd spoken with someone new. *Was* he someone new? She had the strangest feeling she'd seen him or met him before. She realized the park was suddenly empty. It was just the two of them alone.

"Thérèse is an interesting character," Lawrence said. "Victim and villain. You don't know if you should love her or hate her."

"I—I'm not there yet," Sarah responded.

"You'll see," he said. "Obviously, she has a choice, but a marriage like that, where you hate the person—it's like being in prison." He checked himself. "Sorry. Sarah, I was just—"

"Wait, how do you know my name?" she asked. "Are you sure we haven't met before?"

Lawrence smiled. "No, we haven't," he said. "It's on your nameplate...there." He reached across and touched her necklace chain. "It's quite beautiful. It suits you."

"It was a gift," she said. What was she doing? At the edges of her consciousness, she felt the sky closing in on her, a heavy curtain waiting to drop. She felt the familiar, irrational panic. *Run. Run.*

Her grasping mind found a handhold. Dr. Robin. Her appointment. "I'm sorry, but I really do have to go. I have an appointment I'm going to be late for."

"Too bad," he said, the same sympathetic smile lighting his face. "It was very nice to meet you, Sarah. I'd be interested in knowing how you feel about Thérèse as you read on. Maybe we can have a Zola book club in the park?"

Sarah smiled and then said, "Maybe?" She stood up, straightening her coat. No more words came. Before he could respond, she turned and walked away. She hoped desperately that no one had been looking at her. Her face felt bright red. There had been a pleasant glitch in her routine, something she felt excited about. She was going to be late after all. There was no way she'd be telling Dr. Robin about this meeting—not today anyway.

It wasn't until she was almost at her therapist's office that she realized she had left her book on the bench.

# CHAPTER 2

*When there is no hope in the future, the
present appears atrociously bitter.*
THÉRÈSE RAQUIN

The receptionist didn't recognize Sarah when she arrived. She
never did. She always looked up her name, every single time,
with the same blank expression. It was impossible to tell whether
she was doing it consciously or not. Sarah sat and opened a
magazine, kicking herself for leaving behind her book.

Sarah remembered Dr. Robin's admonition: "*Try not to use
those words: 'Always,' 'never,' 'you always,' 'you never.' 'Impossible.'
'Every time.'*" They were so difficult to cut out of her vocabulary,
those aggressive, brittle words. But the therapist was right, as
always. Non-violent communication was key to normalizing
emotions, getting them under control.

Helena Robin seemed to have mastered that particular technique. She always seemed to deal with pain, suffering, chaos, and confusion as though they were entirely normal feelings, emotional experiences as ordinary as boredom or hunger. She was especially adept at defusing anger. Sarah wondered sometimes if she was even human.

"Don't you just want to *give up* sometimes?" Sarah had once asked her. The calm, collected empathy of the therapist's response had partly soothed, partly infuriated her. Now she only asked it in her mind, along with many other questions. Their relationship, though powerful in its depths of trust and openness, sometimes seemed a fragile shell that was up to Sarah to keep intact.

Dr. Robin had been referred to Sarah by her friend, Laura, back when Sarah had first started experiencing blackout periods and those awful nightmares. Sarah was reluctant, but she had to admit that the incidents were affecting everyone and everything in her life. Laura, who'd been to see the therapist for some kind of postpartum care, had strongly suggested that Sarah give Dr. Robin a try. To her surprise, when Sarah brought up the idea with Eric, he'd insisted on it.

Sarah looked around the spotless waiting area, unnerved by the perfect tidiness of the place. It always felt as if she was the doctor's only patient, though she knew that wasn't the case. She'd seen other men and women come through, anonymous figures who smiled apologetically or made halfhearted attempts to shield their faces as they hurried past. She'd been concerned in the beginning that the proximity of the office to her own home would lead to awkward run-ins, but fortunately she'd never seen anyone she recognized.

Dr. Robin, as her patient-friendly website pronounced, specialized in anxiety disorders and fears. Her "About Me" page featured a photo of the attractive, auburn-haired doctor, an appropriately inquisitive expression lighting up her hazel eyes, sitting on a bench somewhere. Underneath her bio were her credentials: M.D. from Cornell, specialization in Psychiatry; internship at Weill-Cornell Hospital in Manhattan; focused studies in psychobiology, the molecular basis of anxiety and psychotic disorders; background in clinical hypnotherapy. It all sounded very impressive to Sarah. But it was Dr. Robin's open face that made her seem most accessible and trustworthy. She also didn't have any social media accounts, which, though unusual, struck Sarah as vaguely healthy. She was on LinkedIn— but that wasn't really social media. Sarah wondered about Dr. Robin's friends and family but never asked.

*"Dr. Robin uses hypnotherapy, in conjunction with traditional therapies, to help her patients transition to a new stage in their lives—one in which they feel empowered to overcome long-lasting fears and anxieties."*

That sounded just right for Sarah; when she read it, she realized she was willing to try anything to accomplish that particular transition. She wasn't sure what the next stage would be, but a part of her life was most definitely over. Eric and the kids reminded her constantly of that.

The hypnosis sessions, as it turned out, were not at all what Sarah had imagined. She had pictured herself floating into a netherworld, like the first time she had smoked pot in her freshman year of college. That experience had been surprisingly blissful: an immersion into a quieter, more accepting place where everything needn't be perfect. Sarah had loved it so much that it had terrified her, and she'd vowed never to do it again.

Hypnosis was different. The first time she'd walked into Dr. Robin's office, she had not felt calm at all; she'd been on edge, as tense as ever. Dr. Robin had sat down and spoken to her in a silky, soothing voice:

"You don't have anything to be afraid of, Sarah. We're not going to do anything you haven't done before in one way or another. Hypnosis is essentially a state of heightened focus and receptivity, with the critical mind in abeyance. During such a state, the subconscious mind is left a bit more open, a bit more receptive and suggestible. It's perfectly natural—in fact, you go in and out of it many times a day. Think of that half-hour before you fall asleep and after you wake up: that's a hypnotic state. You could think of it in terms of creativity, or freedom of thought—that hypnotic state right before you fall asleep is often when the most interesting ideas will occur to you."

Sarah wasn't sure what Dr. Robin meant at first. But after a session, she realized that hypnosis didn't involve self-abandonment or paralysis or anything like that. It was just being in touch with herself on a deeper level, a level she didn't always reach normally. During the sessions, she hardly knew she was under hypnosis; she felt entirely in control of herself and had to be assured by Dr. Robin that a change had even taken place.

She had been feeling better since coming to Dr. Robin. Now she attended regular sessions with the therapist and even almost looked forward to them sometimes. More than anything, the routine comforted her; it felt good to have the solidity of that schedule to rely upon. Still, the time leading up to each session was always fraught with anxiety.

Today was no better. The barrage of feelings aroused by the

stranger in the park had subsided into a vague annoyance with her own lack of self-control. She couldn't remember the last time someone showed interest in her. Surely it wouldn't kill her to indulge the friendly overtures of a stranger once in a while, especially one so handsome. Judging from the wait, she certainly needn't have hurried away so quickly on her therapist's account.

* * *

"Dr. Robin will see you now," the receptionist called out. As always, she said it without looking up. *Rude.* The aggressive word felt good, so she said it out loud.

"Rude."

"What was that?" the receptionist asked, finally looking up to acknowledge her.

Sarah coughed, giggling to herself. "Nothing at all," she smiled at the receptionist.

She entered the therapist's empty office. She looked around the room. As with the ultra-clean waiting area, everything in Dr. Robin's office was white—clean and crisp, like a clear mind. Only the windows offered any respite from the room's starkness. The lack of photos or art had always made her nervous, though she understood the significance. It didn't matter how many sessions she had: in this place, she always felt messy, as though her dark thoughts were visible blotches, or ragged encumbrances hanging off of her.

At least, that's how she always felt at first. And it was probably part of the point; it kept her focused on those disorderly thoughts, on accepting them and letting them go. *You are your mind; your mind is not you*—the phrase had sounded like psychobabble when Dr. Robin had first mentioned it, but now

Sarah often found herself returning to it, almost as a mantra. The repetition was soothing, a version of her own voice that grounded her rather than fighting her.

"Your inner voice should be a friend, not an enemy," the doctor had told her. "You wouldn't keep someone around you who was negative all the time, would you? Let's find you a new inner friend."

She relaxed into the soft white couch, bringing her breathing under control. She thought of calm places, of pleasant, clean things: the kids on the beach, little again, collecting shells; Eric with his surfboard, the saltwater in his hair. No one ever told you to hold onto those moments while they were happening; no one ever said how hard it would be to enjoy them once they were just memories.

*You are your mind; your mind is not you.*

"Hi there, Sarah," Dr. Robin's calm voice entered the room with her. "I'm so sorry to keep you waiting."

The therapist sat down in her chair across from Sarah, a journal in her lap. She looked kind and understanding as always, her hair smooth and impeccably pulled back. Her features had always struck Sarah as oddly aristocratic, even regal: a straight nose and proud chin to go with her upright posture. She wasn't tall—much shorter than Sarah, in fact—but in the chair, sitting up as she did, she never failed to look bigger. Her clothes were always neutral-colored with some small accent of color. Today she wore a cream-colored skirt and jacket with a little bird pin in the lapel, a robin, no doubt, with a ruby eye—a little quirkier than usual, but disarmingly cute nonetheless.

"You look better today, if I may say so," she smiled. "Do you feel better than when I last saw you?"

THE WOMAN IN THE PARK

"I guess so, a bit," Sarah said diffidently. They always began their sessions this way, just talking, but this time felt different. She wasn't ready to get into anything just yet. "I walked over. The fall air feels good."

Sarah thought of Jason and Darcy, playing in the leaves. "The kids are home early tonight, too, so I'm looking forward to that."

"Right—boarding school," Dr. Robin said. "I remember you telling me you had some mixed feelings about that before. Does seeing them on the weekends make that any easier to deal with?"

"It can. It's kind of a tradeoff, though. The rest of the time…I'm sometimes more down than I would be otherwise." She shifted uncomfortably in her seat. "It's hard for me when they're away. Harder than I expected it would be, really. But we—ah—well, he feels that it's best for them. Eric does." Her voice already sounded like somebody else's, faraway and quiet. She looked down at her hands in her lap, at her chewed fingernails. *I have to quit the bad habits,* she thought. What other ones did she have?

"I see," said Dr. Robin, "and what about you?"

"Me? I never really think about what I want."

"Do you think it's best for them? As you say Eric does?"

Sarah thought of the kids coming out of school with their backpacks and winter jackets, now so big. They seemed to change so much while they were away from her. She shrugged. "I guess so. It's hard to say right now; I think I confuse it with how it makes me feel most of the time."

"Which is?"

"Well, there are positives and negatives."

"What would you say are the positives?"

"It definitely leaves me with a lot more time for myself."

"What do you do with it?"

Sarah thought a moment. "I spent some time in the park today. Most of the time…well, I don't know." She picked at her fingernails. *Might as well get it out there*, she thought. "I spent last night going through Eric's things," she admitted.

"Oh, Sarah," Dr. Robin's veneer cracked for an instant; her concern was visible, almost maternal. "Again?"

"Yes."

"What did you expect to find?"

*Come on*, Sarah thought. *Forty percent of married men cheat on their wives, and you're asking me what I expected to find?*

"Proof," she said.

"Proof?"

"Yeah, proof. Hairs, makeup stains. I don't know, anything."

Dr. Robin sighed. "And did you find any?"

Sarah shook her head.

"As you didn't the last time."

"Yeah."

"But you still feel the need to look for it."

"Apparently."

Sarah looked at the doctor, impatient to change the subject.

"I'm still having those nightmares," she blurted out.

"Nightmares?"

At least Dr. Robin sounded interested.

"You'll have to remind me—which nightmares do you mean?"

"Same as I always have," Sarah sighed. "Eric and Juliette. It's always them."

"You know it's only a dream," Dr. Robin reassured her.

"And then I'm running, always running from something.

Or to something," she said. "There's nothing there to run to, or from. Ever."

The therapist opened her journal and made a few notes. "What do you mean, nothing there?" she asked.

"I am running. I'm outside, I'm wet, and it's cold. And then the sky flashes and then there is thunder and a loud crash, then a scream and all goes dark."

"What do you make of it?"

"It's scary, and I feel alone."

"Of course. No one likes to have nightmares, though you know as well as I do that they can't do anything to you. They aren't real, they are a manifestation of how you feel, of your thoughts," Dr. Robin explained. "Can we talk a little about your parents?"

Sarah looked around feeling very vulnerable. "You were asking how I feel about the kids being in boarding school."

"Yes, but first let's talk about your mother and your father," Dr. Robin insisted.

Sarah looked at her firmly, "I don't want to talk about them. They were good parents, and they died when I was young."

"Were they?"

Sarah persisted, "Yes, they were a great couple. I only wish Eric and I were more like them."

Dr. Robin took notes in her journal.

"You asked me about boarding school," Sarah reminded her, changing the subject.

"Sure." Dr. Robin nodded encouragingly.

"If I'm being completely honest, I don't like it at all. In fact, I hate it."

"What do you hate about it?"

"It just feels unnatural. I mean, I want them with me, all the time. I know I can't have that, but I want it. And when they come home on weekends, I feel distant from them. I just keep thinking of how things used to be. This way—I don't know, it's like they're gone. Like they've left, and Eric's left, and I'm just left behind."

"I understand."

"Do you?" Sarah felt her voice rise in response to a sudden heat within her.

"Of course. What you're talking about is loss. Everyone can understand that on some level."

"What have *you* lost?" Sarah said, raising her voice again. Isn't that what these sessions were supposed to be teaching her? "Do you have kids in boarding school? Do you even have kids?"

"You know that isn't the point here, Sarah."

"That's right, you never answer any of *my* questions," Sarah muttered. She looked at her fingernails again. Dr. Robin let the silence hang, expecting her to go on. It always frustrated Sarah when she did that, though her expression now was not unkind. "He *is* seeing someone," she went on, without looking up. "Eric is always out late, or needing to be somewhere else in a hurry, or just not at home at all. That's why I keep looking through his things. It's not jealousy. I can feel him acting different with me. He's too busy for the kids, too busy for me," Sarah sighed. "He's never present."

"Never? Remember, that kind of unqualified language is rarely accurate, right?"

"Fair enough, but it's still true in this case."

"And you feel this absence because he's having an affair and no other reason? You've thought that before, remember?" Dr.

Robin said calmly.

"And now it's really true." Sarah looked out the window. She knew how she sounded; it was impossible to convey the utter simplicity of it. "I know it is. I saw him with Juliette. He didn't know I was there, but they were having lunch together. I watched them. I saw how he looked at her."

Dr. Robin wrote a bit more in her journal. Sarah hated that journal. She constantly wondered what was in it.

"I can't blame him, I guess," Sarah reflected. "She *is* young and pretty."

"And you don't feel that way yourself?"

Sarah cringed inwardly. "No."

"Well, that's something we might spend some time with in our session today," the therapist said. "I should tell you that these are normal feelings—especially for women as they get older, and most especially for women with children. But for now—leaving aside the question of whether Eric is or isn't having an affair in reality—can you tell me specifically how that thought, the thought that he *is* doing that, makes you feel?"

"I almost can't allow myself to think about it," Sarah heard herself say. "It makes me too angry."

"Too angry in what sense?"

"Like it would make me lose control."

"And do something?"

"Maybe, yeah," Sarah admitted.

"What are you worried it would make you do?"

It was the kind of thing Dr. Robin always seized on. But Sarah knew better than to answer that honestly. There were limits to patient confidentiality.

"I haven't thought that far ahead," she said.

ENTRY, OCTOBER 11, 2018
Patient: Sarah Rock
Age: 39 (Dob: 12/7/1978)

Sarah continues to be a classic case of mood-congruent disorders, specifically related to loss trauma.

She exhibits the most acute signs of paranoia and distress when talking about her husband, Eric. I have tried on many occasions to help her reconcile these feelings with other losses in her life, but she tends to respond belligerently. She believes that Eric has been cheating on her with his younger coworker, Juliette, and has tried in vain on numerous occasions to produce proof of the affair. She doesn't go into any potentially dangerous specifics, but has admitted to following Eric and Juliette, which does concern me, especially in light of what has happened in the past.

She also misses her two children, who are away at boarding school, and has lost her sense of purpose. She reports recurrent nightmares: absent-space pursuits, disembodied figures. I am trying hypnosis and cognitive therapy along with medications.

I suspect she is no longer taking the latter as directed, but she insists that she is. Her use of unqualified language is becoming more frequent and associated with her distorted perceptions of Eric and Juliette. I have been coaxing her to not use words like 'never' and 'always' in her speech patterns. I hope she can understand the reasons for my suggestions.

# CHAPTER 3

*Thérèse, who had not yet pronounced a word, looked at the new arrival. She had never seen such a man before. Laurent, who was tall and robust, with a florid complexion, astonished her. It was with a feeling akin to admiration that she contemplated his low forehead planted with coarse black hair, his full cheeks, his red lips, his regular features of sanguineous beauty.*

THÉRÈSE RAQUIN

Even without Dr. Robin's interrogations, it was hard for her to say how she spent her time. With this much time to herself, it would seem that the hours would drag by; but most of the time when she wasn't asleep, the hours flew by instead. It was one of the drawbacks of therapy days, in particular, that sometimes her mind would feel disorganized, unfamiliar, as though someone else had been moving furniture around in there.

Still, Sarah knew it was all for the greater good. It took work to get better.

Deciding to stay out, she took a long walk up Fifth Avenue along Central Park, feeling the difference the day had made.

Her session that morning had energized her, and the heaviness had cleared in the cool autumn air; the afternoon sun seemed to embrace her. She passed the Ukrainian Institute on the corner of 79th Street with its big windows and balcony, its long curtains hiding the memories of the family that once lived there. She walked by the New York Society Library, where she often read, and resisted the urge to go inside.

Fishing in her bag for her sunglasses, she narrowly avoided running into a pretty young woman, who responded to her apology with a huff as she walked off. The girl reminded her of Juliette: petite, dark eyes, not a wrinkle or blemish on her. Sarah shook off the darkness that threatened to creep back up on her from the inside. She really had no reason to suspect her husband; it was her he loved, not Juliette.

On Madison Avenue, heading towards home, she stopped by the Goddess International Delicatessen, a fancy deli with specialties from around the world. The Goddess was one of her housewifely tricks, a little white lie she shared with a number of other moms in the neighborhood. A few dishes from here, heated up and paired with a salad, never failed to look like the perfect homemade meal, whipped up by a magic mom. The kids would never know. Even Eric thought she was a great cook. On many occasions it had proven to be an absolute lifesaver.

When she arrived home, Manuel was still at the front, his shift not yet over. He held the door for her as she hurried in.

"Party in 8B tonight," he said, taking her bags and placing them in the elevator. "Call us if it's too loud, okay?"

"Thanks, Manuel," she said, noting again the look of sympathy in the doorman's face.

The apartment was shockingly cold, almost icy. No

Eric—but that was hardly a surprise. She went to the thermostat and turned up the heat. She wished she had time for a hot bath, but with the kids coming home early this afternoon it would have to wait.

Sarah carried the food down the long hallway to the kitchen and placed the bags on the marble counter. The kitchen felt stark and empty. She took out fruit from one bag and placed it in a big bowl. The color cheered up the lonely room, just a bit. She turned on the oven and poured herself a glass of sauvignon blanc. If the bath wasn't happening for now, at least this was.

She touched the nameplate on her necklace, thinking again of her encounter in the park, of that mysterious handsome stranger who shared her love of the classics. What was his name? Lawrence. She remembered how her stomach had fluttered when he'd said her name. She had to admit, he was attractive. Maybe even more so than Eric, if she was being honest.

She checked the oven and looked at the clock, registering the time with surprise. The kids—any minute now. She looked at her phone; no messages or texts. Had she been waiting for someone to call?

Smiling at her own absent-mindedness, she juiced lemons and chopped up an onion, seeded a pomegranate, put the fish in the oven and the sauce and kale on burners to heat up, and added a bit more white wine to the sauce—and a bit more for herself, while she was at it. Even keeping up the illusion of domestic mastery held a certain charm for her.

She heard the front door slam shut, followed by the sound of heavy bags dropping to the floor. Immediately the house felt warmer to her, a home again.

"Jason? Darcy?" she called. "Hi, sweethearts!"

Her son shuffled in first. Her oldest, her handsome boy, the one who had first taught her heart to love unconditionally. He seemed older every time she saw him; somehow, he was almost as tall as she was now. She shoved down a pang of melancholy and kissed him.

"Hey, Mom." Jason looked at her, his blue eyes piercing. For an instant he seemed to be searching for something in her face—then it passed. "Smells good," he sniffed; then flashed by her down the hallway. She heard the door to his room shut. A few moments later the inevitable music was playing.

Fourteen years old and he was already gone. She felt a sudden rush of helplessness and heard Dr. Robin's voice: "The words matter; they become the way you think. Try to give the feelings better words, words that will help rather than hurt you." Jason wasn't gone—he was just living his own life. She wasn't helpless—it was just hard to adjust to change sometimes. No one had ever told her that being a parent involved so much loss—all that significance a child would never understand, so wonderful and frightful at the same time.

Sarah resisted the urge to follow Jason and instead went to the foyer to meet Darcy. Her little girl was struggling out of her coat, already showing the monumental exasperation only felt by twelve-year-olds.

"Hi, sweetie," Sarah said, moving in to help her.

Darcy shrugged her off. "Mom, I've got it," she snapped. Finally getting through the zipper, she threw the coat down onto her backpack with a huff and smiled wearily.

"Welcome home, princess." Sarah held her close, reveling in her daughter's still-unresisting embrace. Pre-teen attitude had come with her move to boarding school, but Darcy was still her little angel. She was just a slightly more-prickly angel these days.

Flicking her long hair out of her face, Darcy started for the kitchen. "What's for dinner?" she asked. "I'm starving! The bus ride was awful."

*At least she's not shutting herself in her room yet*, Sarah thought. She thought of calling Eric, but a jealous twinge checked her. Let him miss out, if he had such other important places to be. The kids were part of what he was missing, too.

\* \* \*

Dinner was soon on the table, and the three of them sat down to eat. She served the meal on Eric's parents' best china; this was as special an occasion as any. Jason turned up his nose at the flounder.

"Fish, huh?" Jason said.

"It's flounder, in a lemon and white wine sauce. I used to make it for you all the time—you don't like it anymore?"

Jason's look was resigned. "Never mind, Mom. It's fine."

Sarah refilled her wine glass. "So how was your week?"

"It was school," Jason said scornfully.

"But I wasn't there. Did anything special happen? For either of you?"

"No," they both said at the same time.

"What about that paper you were working on, Jason?" Sarah tried again. "You turned that in this week, right?"

"Yeah. I got an A on it."

"That's fantastic!"

"Whatever," Jason gave her a blank look. "It was easy."

"Still, that's great. I know you took it seriously."

He picked distractedly at his kale. She wondered if he was

still having trouble making friends at school. *Better let Eric fish for that one*, she thought.

"What about you, Darcy?" she asked her daughter. "Are you liking school any better?"

"Not much," Darcy said. "Kind of, sometimes."

"Are you at least sleeping better?"

"Ugh, no. The beds are stiff and always smell weird."

"I'll have to call them about that," Sarah said, resisting the temptation to laugh. For all her whining, Darcy seemed so serious these days. "I couldn't sleep on a weird-smelling bed either."

"Can't we go somewhere closer, so we can sleep here again?"

"We're only a month in, stupid," Jason said.

"Jason." She turned back to Darcy. "We're giving this a try for now, honey. If it doesn't work out, we'll change it."

"I hate boarding school," Darcy pouted.

"I know, baby. But your dad and I—Hey! Jason, I said no phones!"

Jason groaned and set his phone down next to his plate. Sarah picked it up to put it behind her on the counter.

"Mom! I'm not using it," he protested.

The phone vibrated in Sarah's hand as she set it facedown on the counter, refusing to look at it. Maybe she didn't have to worry about the two of them making friends after all. *Give the feelings better words.* "Come on, I haven't seen you two all week. Here I am, living the same old boring life, and you've got nothing new to tell me?"

Darcy looked embarrassed. "Sorry, Mom. It's just school. It's boring too."

Sarah started to say something, but looked at Jason and

stopped.

He was glaring at the empty chair with the place setting.

"Why do you do that?" he asked quietly, motioning at Eric's chair.

Sarah flinched. "What? Set a place for your dad?"

"Yeah," Jason said. He was looking at her now, his face imploring. "Why do you even act like he's coming?"

"Why wouldn't I?"

"Because you know he's not."

She flushed with embarrassment and anger at her husband. She and Eric had talked countless times about the importance of eating together, of being there together to greet the kids when they came home. Boarding school was already such a burden on them. How could he have let himself become so distant that even the kids could see it?

"I—it's a habit," she heard herself say.

"Are you serious?" Despite his gentler voice, Jason's look was equal parts pity and contempt, a grotesque mixture in a face so young. "Come on, Mom. You need to stop it."

Her cheeks burned. "I know," she said. "I—I knew he had to be away, Jason. I just—I'm sorry. I was just hoping it would be different this time."

Jason stared at her, disbelieving. She felt her heart break at the look in his eyes. Wasn't there something else there, too—something still more vulnerable, still more strangely adult? Finally he looked away.

"Whatever," he said. "It's fine, Mom. Just—you don't have to do that." His voice softened. "We get it."

A wave of sadness ran through her, and she fought back tears. She looked at Darcy, who was staring into her lap. This was all going wrong. She'd been so excited to see the kids, and now she'd upset both of them. *Goddamn it, Eric.* It was beyond unfair; it was nothing they should have to deal with. Ever.

"I have a treat for you guys," she ventured, desperate to lighten the mood. "We've got pumpkin pie for dessert, with whipped cream."

Darcy brightened. Jason breathed a heavy sigh.

How could it have become so difficult to tell what he was thinking? *Let it drop, Mom.* Solid ground again—the voice of teenage impatience, or so she hoped. "You're not going to tell me you don't like that, either?" she teased.

Jason smiled just a bit, in spite of himself. "It's not natural to eat something that looks like a person's head," he said.

The relief was incredible. "Now you're just trying to be difficult," she managed to say lightly. "Darcy, what about you? You'll eat a little jack-o'-lantern, won't you?"

Darcy giggled. "Yeah," she said.

"It's a special occasion, after all." Sarah got up to clear the plates. "If you guys want, we can watch a movie after. Whatever you want."

"Yeah!" Darcy said exuberantly.

Even Jason seemed willing to give in a little. "Sure, that sounds good," he said.

This time when his phone buzzed again, on her way to the kitchen, she didn't mind.

* * *

The evening after, the kids were both away, sleeping over at friends' places in the city, while Sarah and Eric got ready to attend a fundraiser. She tried to make peace with the fact that everyone was living such separate lives these days.

She'd waited up for Eric after the children had gone to bed the night before, but had been too tired to quarrel with him when he finally came home. They'd agreed to spend the morning together with Jason and Darcy, but she had been exhausted and overslept. When she woke in the late morning, Eric was gone again.

Nevertheless she'd managed to spend a pleasant afternoon with them but found it unsettling how reticent they were about the morning they'd spent with their father. It was as though they were protecting their relationship with him from her, or perhaps protecting her from it; they each seemed unwilling to go into it with her, as though cautious of some hidden volatility.

She went into her oversized closet, leafed through her clothes. Everything was in order, just the way she liked it, orga-nized by color, every shade of the rainbow with whole sections at the end for those staple colors of Manhattan nightlife: white and black. Feeling like wearing black, she chose a simple black sheath, carefully applied her makeup and opened her jewelry box. She withdrew the nameplate necklace again, briefly remem-bering the way the stranger in the park had touched it. Had it really only been a day since then?

She shook the thoughts from her mind, concentrating on the necklace instead. Eric had bought it for her the year before Jason was born, in Colombia, when they'd gone to Cartagena for a wedding. She'd loved the seaside town with its hint of danger, its spicy food, its side streets and small shops full of local art, jewelry, and strong coffee. One night, the electricity had gone out in the entire area and blackness had descended over the town. The streets had all looked the same to them, unfamiliar and rough, and they'd nearly been hit by a motorcycle roaring out of an alley. Even Eric had had a nervous smell about him as they'd returned to their hotel room. It had felt dangerous and sexy, and that night they'd made love like never before, with a sense of urgency that she still remembered. Sarah had thought there would be many more trips to come like that one: wild and carefree. Shortly thereafter, however, Jason was born, and the trips became less carefree, then less frequent, then they stopped altogether.

She slipped into the dress, feeling its silky coolness caress her back as she zipped it up. As usual, she was naked underneath—she hated wearing panties or bras and preferred going without them when she could. She remembered how, when she'd told Dr. Robin about this, the therapist had cocked her head and written it down in her notebook. Had the idea surprised her? Sarah secretly hoped so. What would Lawrence think, she wondered—then dismissed the thought with a smile.

She heard a footstep on the bedroom floor and Eric was there again with her, elegant in his dark blue suit and crisp white shirt. She felt his hands on her back and, as angry as she had been at him all day, part of her anger dissolved into sadness and desire. He looked much as he had in Cartagena; did he still see her as he had then?

"I like it when you're home," she said. "So do the kids."

"I know." He kissed her gently. She could smell his cologne, the same that he'd worn when they'd first met and only wore when they went out together: French vetiver, leather and spice. It smelled of anticipation to her. "*Très jolie, ma belle*—are you ready?"

She loved it when he spoke French to her. But today it felt like a distraction.

"The kids missed you last night at dinner," she said.

"I know. I missed them, too."

*But not me*, she thought. "Jason seemed angry," she went on, brushing aside her rage, "and I'm sure Darcy will be following suit soon enough."

"They're kids," Eric said. "They'll be all right if we are."

Sarah looked hard at him. "And are we?" she asked.

"Of course we are." He kissed her again, running his hands up her neck, over her necklace, through her hair. It sent shivers up her spine as it always had. How could she even entertain the thought of another man with Eric here? A sickening guilt overcame her and she wanted to forgive everything, wanted him to make love to her like he had in Colombia, when the lights went out and the dangers of the world were just another adventure they were on together.

\* \* \*

They joined friends at the museum bar. The soirée—a fundraiser for education in underserved communities—was well attended, and a buzz filled the room, making it feel like the place to be. Wannabe-famous people, maybe-famous people, and even a few bona fide celebrities had turned out, most of them rich, spoiled men and women looking to top each other in generosity—just as they topped each other on where they vacationed and how big their houses were.

Sarah had regretted coming as soon as they'd arrived. Her friend Laura, who'd extended the invitation to her, was nowhere to be seen and the music was overloud, reducing conversation to shouted pleasantries. Sarah and Eric made their way to the bar where she ordered a red wine while he glanced around the room.

Eric was distracted, impatient. A few times she reached for his hand but he moved away too quickly, called to conversations elsewhere. Soon she felt alone, forgotten in the midst of small talk with people she barely knew.

Then she saw the woman standing at the other end of the bar.

*Juliette.*

She was perfect, the height of youthful splendor. She wasn't as tall as Sarah, but that didn't matter—Juliette's firm, unwrinkled skin, shiny ebony hair, perky breasts, and elegant neck were everything Sarah's own body wasn't. Sipping her drink, her long, dark hair cascading gracefully over her shoulders, the young woman looked as though she could have anything she wanted, simply by commanding it.

It couldn't be a coincidence. Eric must have told Juliette they would be there.

Sarah felt the blood rush to her face. Before she could stop herself, she approached Juliette, as if on a mission. Sarah could smell the lilac aroma of her perfume, and it was nauseating.

"Juliette?"

Juliette turned with a surprised face. "Hi, Mrs. Rock."

Sarah glanced at the group she was with, and they were all looking at her.

"I didn't realize you would be here," Sarah said.

"My friend volunteers for the committee, and she invited some of us," Juliette explained.

Sarah nodded, even though inside she knew Juliette was lying. Before anyone could see how upset she was, she escaped toward the back of the bar and ducked into the ladies' room, rushing past two women at the sink to lock herself in a stall. She breathed in and out, slowly, just as Dr. Robin had instructed her to do, counting silently to five: *One, two, three, four…*

Darkness lapped at the corners of her mind, coming closer. The room felt as though it was getting smaller, warmer; a strange heat burned in her chest and spread up through her neck. She touched her cheeks, felt the skin there growing fierier with every moment. The other women's voices sounded incoherent and faraway. It seemed they would never leave.

Once they were gone, she emerged and rinsed her face with cold water, forcing herself to keep breathing deeply. Slowly the fire within her cooled, and her heartbeat slowed down. Looking up, she saw herself in the mirror, wide-eyed and panicked.

Over her shoulder, she saw a figure stir in the shadows behind her.

She jumped and turned around. No one was there. She could have sworn it was a person, though no one she knew—a figure like one from her dream, uncoiling itself from the darkness like a snake. Slowly she turned back to look in the mirror again; she was alone.

How dare Eric make her feel this way! She wasn't going to let the two of them make a fool of her for another minute. She rushed out of the restroom, her hands still wet, to find him.

ENTRY, OCTOBER 16, 2018
Patient: Sarah Rock
Age: 39 (Dob: 12/7/1978)

This morning Sarah exhibited unusual hostility during our session. She sat in silence for almost the entire hour, despite my attempts at different conversational topics. She seems to be looking for something to validate her anger. For the most part I didn't engage with her, instead allowing her to sit in silence. She was also wearing deep-red lipstick, a shade she doesn't usually wear—and one that she has remarked on before as being particularly disliked by her husband.

She is evidently going through a transformation, some new realization, though she's not yet ready to share it with me. She is defying authority, with me as the representative of that authority; it is obviously part of the process. I'm giving her the space to figure it out; hopefully she'll respond by coming to her next session. If she does, we'll try to see what this newfound anger is all about.

CHAPTER 4

*The nature of the circumstances seemed to have made this woman for this man, and to have thrust one towards the other. The two together, the woman nervous and hypocritical, the man sanguineous and leading the life of a brute, formed a powerful couple allied. The one completed the other, and they mutually protected themselves. At night, at table, in the pale light of the lamp, one felt the strength of their union, at the sight of the heavy, smiling face of Laurent, opposite the mute, impenetrable mask of Thérèse.*
THÉRÈSE RAQUIN

What was she doing in the park again?

Her kids were gone, back at school for another week; she didn't belong among all these young, hopeful moms and their bubbly kids—crying, laughing, and growing up right before everyone's eyes. But then, that wasn't why she was here anyway.

Her eyes went to the bench where she'd been sitting the other day. Nothing. No book. No Lawrence. She felt relief and disappointment, and the desire to give in to guilty pleasure. She sat down, a solitary onlooker.

Why couldn't Eric see that it was his fault she felt this way? But then, that was the problem—it was up to her to see everything, to know everything. Their fight the night before was still ringing in her ears, but for him it was just another exchange of words on his way out the door.

It was partly her fault, as it always was; the amount she'd drunk made it easier for him to dismiss her accusations. She looked back on the years with the same puzzlement she'd always felt; it all happened so quickly.

For the first few years, anyway, things had been blissful. They'd been inseparable; it was the pure, reliable love she'd been waiting for her whole life. Both of them had been crazy about each other; they talked and made love for hours, unable to get enough of one another. They married young—he proposed on her twenty-fourth birthday—and for some time, the passion had continued unabated.

Admittedly, when the kids came, Sarah found excuses not to have sex; postpartum depression, weariness, simple stress over the degree of change. But though he was frustrated, Eric had been patient with her—even more patient with her than she was with herself. When her depression deepened after Darcy was born, and turned to fits of helpless despair when breastfeeding didn't take, Eric did everything he could to support the family.

But there was another reversal ahead. One day, the depression lifted like a heavy fog dispersing, and she suddenly felt back to normal. Her sex drive leaped again, to heights she hadn't even known before, waiting for Eric to come home. At first he was thrilled with her newfound fervor, but then something shifted. He began to back away from her and came up with his own excuses to leave her wanting. He spent more time at work and on the road. Her depression returned and with it the nightmares and obsessive thoughts. Eric was completely distant now. When

Sarah met Juliette, she knew the reason.

Now he was off in Boston, away on another trip—with his mistress, no doubt. His position at the bank had changed over the past 10 years, and now he was a managing director and had to be away a lot more. He had long since given up even lying to Sarah about Juliette being along on these work trips, and admitted it openly, as if the fact that she worked for him made their little affair any less transparent.

Sarah heard a child's laugh. She watched the mother from the other day playing with her son. Sarah noticed the woman and her friend looking back at her.

She couldn't remember what she was still doing there. The playground area was no place for adults without children—even those who had once been mothers.

* * *

She stopped in at the Neighborhood Bookstore, that cozy maze of quiet shelves where she could hide, leafing through other people's ideas, other people's feelings. Places like this reminded her that she was only a small piece of a larger puzzle. Her eyes scanned the shelves but the titles were unintelligible to her; as though the names were shifting back and forth. It was the medication, affecting her concentration as it always did. She made a mental note to cut back on it again.

"May I help you find something?" A clerk had appeared at her side.

"*Thérèse Raquin*," she heard herself say. "Do you happen to have a copy? I seem to have misplaced mine."

"Émile Zola." The clerk scanned the shelf, shook his head. "*Raquin*—it's one of his darker novels. I don't believe we have it in stock right now, though we have some other works by Zola here. I can order it for you?"

Sarah shook her head, strangely confused. "No, that's fine, thanks. I can always order it myself. I just thought I'd give it a try, since I was in the area."

She walked out empty-handed and continued down the block to the corner supermarket. Dinner—that was useful. Entering, she walked up and down the aisles aimlessly, placing items in her basket. At the checkout counter, she looked down to find almonds, berries, seaweed crackers, three bottles of wine. She laughed to herself. She'd have to stop by the gourmet deli again and pick up a proper dinner.

As she was leaving, the sight of a woman approaching from up the street caused her to look away abruptly. Laura—happy, successful Laura, of the perfect kids, the wonderful husband, and the Montauk beach house. A sweet woman, and much more genuine than the average rich Upper East Sider, but about the last person Sarah wanted to see at the moment. Sarah buried herself in her phone and kept walking, but it was too late. Her friend's chipper voice accosted her.

"Sarah. Sarah!"

She turned reluctantly, forcing a smile. Laura looked great as always, tight yoga pants showing off her figure.

"Hey, I thought that was you."

"Hi Laura!" Sarah hoped she sounded surprised and happy to see her. They cheek-kissed. "Sorry, I'm off in my own little world today."

Laura's smile softened with concern. "You left the other night without saying anything—was everything okay?"

"I was just feeling a little off. Too many people, you know

how it is," Sarah said.

Laura toyed with the wide gold cuff on her wrist, a piece she was never without. Sarah had always thought it looked a bit like armor on her slender wrist. "How are Jason, and darling Darcy? Owen said that Jason seems to like boarding school."

"Yes. They like it." Jason and Laura's son, Owen, had been friends since preschool and talked all the time.

"And you?" Laura asked.

"It gives me a lot more time to myself. It's not too far from the country house, which gives me an excuse to get up there more often."

Laura smiled. "That's really good to hear."

Sarah forced a smiling nod. "I've got to get going," she said. She held out her grocery bags and laughed awkwardly. "Still have to pick up some things for dinner."

Laura looked down at the bottles of wine sticking out of Sarah's bags.

She gave Sarah a serious look. "Hey, call me sometime? I'd love to catch up."

Sarah nodded as she slipped past her friend. She knew she wouldn't be calling Laura anytime soon.

\* \* \*

She bought groceries, dropped them off at home, and wandered back out. Though the apartment was large and spacious, she still craved open space, the cold air, and the crowded streets of Manhattan where she could feel alone and not alone.

She walked down Park Avenue, passing by planters with trees in autumn colors: burning red, persimmon orange, ochre yellow. The rain hung in the clouds above her; at each palatial building entrance, doormen stood on guard with umbrellas for whichever privileged tenants might emerge from approaching cars and taxis. She nearly tripped over a dog-walker's confusion of leashes; crossing over to Fifth Avenue, she felt baffled by the swarms of tourists wandering toward their collective destinations. She thought of the herds of sheep she'd seen on a summer trip to the Greek isles, the way Eric had delighted her and the children with sheep calls.

She continued several blocks down Fifth to the Metropolitan Museum. She loved the big building, filled with the beauty and culture and history of the world; just the sight of its massive columns and gracefully ascending steps put her mind at ease. When she was a little girl she'd dreamed of being able to visit the museum just once; now she visited regularly.

The exhibit of Michelangelo's drawings was still up, and she wandered through the museum to peruse it again. Her eyes had to adjust to the darkness and the rhythm of the exhibition— twisted bodies, beauty in ugliness, heads and hands, Mother Mary, the infant Jesus, attending angels. Whole worlds from nothing: eternal beauty from a piece of paper and a chunk of charcoal, a canvas and color, a slab of stone.

How could a man living in Florence 500 years ago bring such calm to the chaos of her mind. And yet that beauty, that Florentine perfection, felt so familiar to her. She had lived in Florence for a semester in college, in a small apartment on a narrow street behind the Uffizi, a five-flight walkup. The stone steps were high, and she'd be sweating and winded when she reached the top. But then, as she opened the door, she would see Florence spread out above the rooftops, breathtaking and serene.

Living among the old buildings and the old ways, she had

felt free and at home. Her decisions had been smaller, and she'd felt braver because of it. She'd bought an old, rickety bicycle and found that people noticed her less when she was riding it. They were, perhaps, the moments she had been most at peace, riding her bicycle over the cobbled streets and soaring bridges. Silently she'd flown through town, observing everything from just the right distance, hiding in plain sight.

It had been a mind-opening, exhilarating time for her—but also lonely. Michelangelo, Botticelli, Giotto and Leonardo Da Vinci had kept her company. She wanted to share the experience with her kids, someday: she would take them to the top of top of Palazzo Vecchio, Florence's town hall, so they could see the view of the city below. She would tell them about the prisoners who had been held in the tower and about the sinister power of the Medici family, so deadly and yet so essential to the legacy of the city. She would point out the hills around the city where the wealthy families had summer villas. She might even tell them about the descendant of one of the ancient Florentine noble families with a murky past, whom she had dated for a few months.

Maybe not.

Continuing through the exhibit, she entered a long dark room and saw the back of a man with a gray jacket. Her hands felt sweaty, and she held her breath as he turned to look at another drawing. She sighed in relief. It was not the man from the park.

\* \* \*

Later, alone at home, Sarah sat at her laptop, a glass of pinot noir—Eric's favorite—close at hand. She took a long gulp, letting the wine warm her throat and insides as she worked her way through emails, making notes on her to-do list.

*Dr. Robin. Country house. Summer plans for the kids.* The summer break was long, almost three months, and she could spend so much of her time planning the activities they needed to fill it: lacrosse, soccer, tennis, dance, guitar and piano lessons, chess, choir, horseback riding. With so many things to do, Sarah worried that her kids would be spread thin. But they never seemed to be.

Busy little bees, she used to call them, and she'd been the queen bee for a while herself: head of her tennis team, hostess of a book club and art club, volunteer at MOMA, chair of the School Outreach program at the Guggenheim, member of the Parents' Association. Keeping busy had always made her feel complete. What had happened to slow her down? Her eyes traveled eagerly to the next item on her list.

*Deal with Eric.*

Sarah looked at the words, confused. Had she written them?

*Deal with Eric.*

She said them out loud, startled by how ominous they sounded. What on earth could she have meant? Confront her husband on his philandering? Gather irrefutable evidence of it? Accept it and move on? Was it another blackout? Sarah wondered.

She felt a presence behind her and froze. Out of the corner of her eye, she glimpsed a shadow, moving past the doorway. Had someone passed behind her? She felt a coldness engulf her as she heard a noise from the living room, a sound of shuffling papers. She shut her computer and got up from the chair.

"Hello?" she called out, not expecting an answer. She looked around the doorway in the direction of Eric's study. Perhaps he'd felt badly about their fight and had come home early.

"Eric? Eric, is that you?"

In the living room, she found the window open. The wind blew through the curtains, flapping them violently. She couldn't remember having opened it. It was the medication, it had to be; there were so many things she didn't remember nowadays.

She closed the window, returned to the bedroom. It seemed like something lurked there still, though she knew that she was alone. Her to-do list lay where she'd left it and that inexplicable line spoke to her, a stranger's words in her own handwriting.

*Deal with Eric.*

She crossed the words out.

\* \* \*

It was appointment day again.

Back in her therapist's office, Sarah was no longer interested in being silent. She needed to talk—and today she felt as though she'd been talking nonstop and taking off one piece of clothing after the other until she stood almost naked in all her ugly glory in front of the doctor.

Sitting there naked might actually have been easier. The doctor's office felt airless and sticky. Sarah's dress felt too tight around the waist, the elastic band pulling at her and reminding her that it was time for a new cleanse. Spinning, running, rumble boxing, Zumba, Pilates—she'd tried them all. Each one had seemed like a cult to her, and a boring cult at that. When she'd told Dr. Robin about her feelings toward group exercise, the therapist had nodded and told her it made sense—telling her that she was running from something, not towards it.

"Have you been drinking?" Dr. Robin asked suddenly, worry in her voice.

"No." She knew the therapist was just doing her job, but she wasn't in the mood to deal with accusations from anyone.

"Sarah," Dr. Robin chided her lightly. "Please—if you're not going to take our work here seriously—"

"Then what?" Sarah took a deep breath. *Defensiveness. Brittleness. Rigidity.* She stood up from her chair. She liked to stand sometimes during her sessions; it gave her a feeling of self-command.

"All right," she admitted. "Fine. I had a glass at lunch, maybe two." In truth she couldn't remember how many she'd had. "That's not such a big deal, is it?"

"You know we can't do any proper hypnotherapy if you've been drinking," the therapist sighed. For an instant Sarah's anger flared, and she wished she'd stayed quiet like last time. "Sarah?"

Sarah shrugged, defiant. "I don't care if we do or don't. It doesn't seem to me that it's working anyway."

"What makes you say that?"

"It's simple," Sarah said. "Nothing is changing. I do the same exact thing practically every day. I get up, have tea and yogurt, go to yoga, go to the park, go to the market, make dinner, see the kids for the weekend, see my husband never. I'm getting sick of this fucking routine. And I'm getting sick of these useless sessions. Once in a while they make me feel better, but it never lasts. It never brings me any resolution."

Dr. Robin didn't flinch but sat studying Sarah calmly, as though she were an insect. She was pretty but so serious; her auburn hair was always tied back neatly in a tight bun or braid, never long and messy like Sarah's often was. Did she ever scream or yell or cry?

"What would count as resolution for you, Sarah?" she asked.

"Goddamn it," Sarah hissed, turning her back in disgust. The therapist's calm questioning infuriated her. Maybe she needed to up the ante—do something really crazy, but what? What would it take to startle her?

"I'm seeing things," she said.

That brought the journal out. "Seeing what?" the therapist asked.

"I thought I saw someone in my apartment. A shadow, I don't know. A person maybe, and at the event the other day. It felt like something was there. Lurking."

"Something?"

"Yeah, like something watching me." Sarah sat back down.

"Was anyone else home?"

"No. Everyone's away. It was just me in the apartment." Sarah's face darkened. "It often is, nowadays. Maybe I should move. I don't really need all that space anymore." Sensing Dr. Robin's imminent question, she got back on topic. "It must be lack of sleep. I haven't been sleeping."

"What about Eric?" the therapist asked.

"What about him?"

"You're sure it's not him?"

"He's gone again. Business. Or at least that's what he says." Before Dr. Robin could take issue with that as she always did, Sarah let it drop: "I met a man in the park."

The doctor remained stoic. "What man? A friend of yours?"

"No. I mean, maybe. He was sitting across from me at the park. I'd never seen him before. It turns out he'd noticed a book I was reading, and… it's silly, really."

"Hardly!" the therapist said. "It must have been important enough for you to mention it. What book were you reading?"

"*Thérèse Raquin.*"

"I read that in college myself. Interesting book."

Sarah could hardly believe it. A crack in the ice—a tangible piece of information. She wondered if she could turn it into more.

"It seems interesting enough," she said. "What do you remember about it?"

"Nothing good comes of their relationship, does it?" The doctor smiled. "I mean, the affair turns into a disaster."

"I'm sure it doesn't have to."

"How do you mean?" Dr. Robin asked.

"I don't know. It's probably not important anyway, not in a real life sense. But I don't know." She paused. "It's just like there was this glitch in the routine," she went on after a moment. "He disrupted it, and I can't stop thinking about it. I mean, we only spoke for five, maybe ten minutes. But it wasn't anything significant." She exhaled loudly. "It's not like I'll ever see him again."

"Did you want to?" Dr. Robin's voice had reassumed its impossibly calm, I-can-question-you-for-hours tone. "See him again?"

Sarah considered the question. Now was when she really needed to be silent. But she couldn't be.

"No, of course not," she said.

Dr. Robin cocked an eye at her. "I won't judge you."

Sarah looked out the window, not sure she should say anything more. Dr. Robin waited.

"Maybe. I'm not sure." Sarah hadn't honestly considered it until now, but now that she said it, she knew she did want to see Lawrence again. It had felt good just to talk to someone who didn't know her.

"I just—I felt like I had a purpose, that day in the park," she said. "It felt as if I knew this guy, even though it was the first time I had ever seen him. Like things were already somehow… in motion there."

If there was anything that could surprise the therapist, this wasn't it.

"Tell me all about it," Dr. Robin said calmly.

ENTRY, OCTOBER 18, 2018
Patient: Sarah Rock
Age: 39 (Dob: 12/7/1978)

Sarah is reporting seeing and hearing things, apparently frequently. Could be related to lack of sleep or the trauma. Still, she seemed clearer today and less angry. She talked about a man from the park, Lawrence, quite a bit. His presence is important to her, even though she doesn't want to admit it to me or to herself. She is drinking noticeably more and may not be taking her medications as instructed.

Some of her facts were contradictory. Eric is still an issue for her. I have been trying to get her to face the situation more clearly. Her fear of separation is more prevalent. She looked well but was hiding her hands quite a lot; I suspect that was to keep me from noticing how far down she's been biting her nails.

# CHAPTER 5

*In the sudden change that had come over her heart, she no longer recognised herself.*
**THÉRÈSE RAQUIN**

The next morning she left the house early and headed to her yoga studio, a tiny neighborhood place on the second floor of a small building on Madison Avenue that smelled of essential oils. You couldn't see it unless you were looking for it—a quality she liked. It was obnoxious the way women seemed to want to announce their fitness habits to the world. To her, it reeked of the desperate need for attention, the desire for approbation. No hip yoga pants and high-end mat for her; she liked to enter in street clothes and change there, feeling the corresponding shift in herself as she suited up for wellness.

As usual she went through the class at the very back of the

studio. The teacher was unlike most she had encountered, with their forced-calm voices and thinly veiled judgments. He liked to dispense droplets of a dour sort of wisdom in between his more usual litany of sarcastic remarks and inappropriate jokes. Despite his gruff demeanor, listening to him made her less depressed. He seemed a living reminder that plenty of people didn't have it together but could be healthy and happy anyway.

After the class, she changed again and walked back over to Central Park. She wondered for just a moment whether *he* would be there. Being there was enough; just crossing over Fifth Avenue she could sense an opening, a broadening-out of spirit in herself, like arriving at the beach on a hot day and feeling the sea's respite only a breath away.

She walked the park's curving paths for a while, denying her curiosity as long as she could. Before she knew it she was back on her favorite bench, responding to emails on her phone. No sign of the man—of Lawrence. It was all right; everything was all right. The leaves trickled down around her, life and death continuing in its cycle.

The thin autumn sun felt good, a slight warmth melting through her hair and down her body. She wanted to hold onto it, to hide it inside like a squirrel gathering acorns for the winter. For a moment, she closed her eyes and let the warmth fill her. The moment slipped into minutes—she lost track of how many.

A cold wind woke her, and she opened her eyes. Her heart skipped.

Lawrence was standing there, even more handsome than he'd been the other day. A strange, sudden happiness engulfed her at the sight of him. She caught his smile, flashed it back at him.

"It's a good place to relax. Or maybe you were just looking for this?" To her amazement, he handed her the book she'd lost. "I didn't know where to find you, so I thought I'd try here again. Guess I got lucky!"

"I—wow, thank you," she said, and took it from him. "I looked for another copy. I thought I'd lost it." She flipped through the book idly, as though checking to see that all the pages were still there.

"I like the notes and dog-ears you left in it," Lawrence said, gesturing toward the book. "Even in that little bit, you like to reflect on what you read."

Sarah felt a sudden embarrassment, not remembering what she'd written in the margins.

"It's so untidy, isn't it?" she laughed. *Like my nails*, she thought. "I should start using a bookmark."

"Not at all!" He smiled. "It means you enjoy what you're reading and want to feel a part of it. Not everything needs to be so tidy. I get that." He pointed to the empty space next to her. "May I sit?"

Sarah moved over. "Sure," she said, hoping her voice didn't betray her excitement. He sat down beside her. She thought he would turn to face her, but instead he leaned back, looking up at the trees.

"I like it here. It's peaceful." He smiled at her again, a boyishly charming smile.

"Don't you have a job? I mean, during the day." It came out sounding impossibly rude, and Sarah immediately regretted it. "Sorry, I didn't mean anything by that."

Still looking up at the trees, he chuckled. "Even if you did mean something by it. I'm a writer, so part of my job is to be out observing people like you."

"So you've been observing me?"

"I guess I have."

She wasn't sure how to take that. "What do you write?"

"Articles, mostly," he said. "And I'm in the middle of my first novel."

Sarah leaned back, his relaxed vibe rubbing off on her, and she laughed.

He looked at her quizzically. "What's that supposed to mean?"

"A handsome stranger, who just happens to be a novelist, too." Sarah smiled. "A bit clichéd, isn't it?"

"Maybe so. But I am. The novelist part, anyway."

"What's the novel about?"

"I don't think I'm ready to share that just yet," he replied. "I mean, it's very personal. But let me get to know you and I'll open up about it. Maybe I'll even let you read it." He smiled. "If you're lucky."

Sarah laughed again, in spite of herself. "An arrogant writer, at that!" she teased. "Not at all a cliché."

"I'm just a bit shy about my work," he said, and then he stood. "Do you want to walk with me?"

To her surprise, she found herself actually considering it. "Walk where?"

"Well, walk and take the train, actually. I want to show you something—a place downtown. Have you been to The Cat and the Owl?"

"No. What's that, a restaurant?"

"No. It's a shop. I think you'll like it."

She furrowed her brow, surprised she was still entertaining

this idea. "How would you know what I like?"

"It's just a hunch," he admitted. "It feels like a sign, running into you again; a little adventure. What do you say? I'll have you back before dinner, I promise." He held out his hand.

The idea was completely crazy. Going somewhere with a stranger- —on the subway? She couldn't remember the last time she'd even taken the subway; she found it too noisy and crowded to be worth the stress. But now it seemed to beckon her, along with this handsome stranger; exciting and dangerous, like that night with Eric in Cartagena. *A little adventure*, as he said.

She knew she had no choice; she was already there, wherever he wanted to take her. She took Lawrence's hand and let him lead the way.

* * *

They stood close, not speaking a word to one another in the crowded train. She observed the people around her in a strange haze, like figures populating the background of a dream.

The crowd drove them closer together, and his hand slid along her leg, sending heat through her. She blushed, and he moved closer. She couldn't contain a quick laugh. Had she met this man before—seen him and forgotten? Had she ever felt this way before?

As they got out she caught a glimpse of herself in the train window. Her hair had come undone in their hurried walk through the station; she looked feral and exotic. Lawrence guided her out to an unfamiliar part of downtown. It was like they had traveled to another city: even the air smelled different, felt lighter. A momentary thought of Eric crossed her mind, and she pushed it away.

"His own fault," she muttered.

"Did you say something?" Lawrence asked. She only shook her head.

The Cat and the Owl, as it turned out, was a small, dusty bookstore. The aisles were tight, the aging shelves heavy with books. It was like entering a jungle of old knowledge. She couldn't believe she'd never been here before.

He guided her gently with a hand at her back. They walked toward the back of the store where a handwritten sign proclaimed Rare Editions. A hunched-over clerk sat beneath the sign, practically as ancient as the books he watched over.

"Don't mind him—he's been there for 200 years," Lawrence whispered into her ear as if reading her mind. She giggled. "Look," he said, pulling her gently by the hand toward a set of glass cabinets. It was like watching a kid in a candy store. "This is my favorite part of the place. I can get lost here. First-edition Hemingway, Proust—even Shakespeare. But here, look at this," he said, reaching past her to pick out a book. He leaned in close, and she could smell his body: salty and fresh, sun, sea and woods.

"Zola—first edition of Thérèse Raquin," he announced proudly.

Sarah beamed, holding the book.

"This is incredible." She wasn't sure if she was talking about the book or him.

"I knew you would think so. It's been here for so long! There's so much to explore here if you have time to really look." The charming smile shone again.

Sarah touched the book gently and smelled the paper— wood and dust. "I must be pretty closed off," she said. "I thought I knew all the good bookstores in the city."

Lawrence took her hand again.

"I've got a confession to make," he said.

She smiled, uncertain.

"I've watched you in the park for a bit. A few times before the other day. That was just the first time you noticed."

Sarah felt her face flush. She was flattered but cautious. "You did? Why?"

"You just seemed...lost. And I was curious about you. I wondered what a woman like you was doing all alone in the park. Then when I saw you reading so intensely, as if no one else was around...I realized I needed to know more about you." He looked intently at her. "I'm sorry, I don't usually do this." He smiled apologetically.

"No, it's all right," she said. "I don't know why, but it is. It's just...you said I seemed lost. Sometimes it feels like I seem that way to everyone." She shook off the subject, looking straight into his eyes. In the dusky obscurity of the bookstore, their deep blue was transfixing.

Without warning he pulled her to him and kissed her. She felt his tongue open her lips, and she let him in, fading away with each caress of his soft tongue. After a moment, she pulled away.

She shivered a bit, covering it with a laugh, as he brushed her hair back from her face.

"We don't know anything about each other," Sarah whispered. It seemed all she could do to let him know how crazy this was. But then he kissed her again, and all her doubts slipped away. This time it was his turn to pull back, and as he did his hand closed around hers, holding the book.

"It's yours," he said.

"What do you mean?" She blushed, confused.

He nodded, pride in his eyes. "I ordered it for you. They had it waiting for me."

"But how did you know that I would come here with you today?" she asked.

"I didn't," he said, shrugging. "But I hoped you would."

# CHAPTER 6

*Laurent was astonished to find his sweetheart handsome. He had*
*never seen her before as she appeared to him then. Thérèse, supple*
*and strong, pressed him in her arms, flinging her head backward,*
*while on her visage coursed ardent rays of light and passionate*
*smiles. This face seemed as if transfigured, with its moist lips and*
*sparkling eyes. It now had a fond caressing look. It radiated. She*
*was beautiful with the strong beauty born of passionate abandon.*

**THÉRÈSE RAQUIN**

After they said goodbye at the subway stop, she watched him
walk away, the afternoon sun on his shoulders. When he had
gone the length of the block, she expected him to turn around,
and he didn't.

She felt a sudden panic. They hadn't exchanged numbers or
even last names; he'd said he wanted to keep it in the moment,
and she hadn't insisted. Expectations killed relationships like
theirs, he had said—and so she had been left with nothing but
the book and the hope that they would find each other again.

She walked up Lexington Avenue alone, feeling as though
she were living someone else's life. Passing a corner store not far

from her building, she saw rows of flowers in all hues. She usually bought white flowers, but this time a bouquet of soft roses in a dark persimmon-orange color beckoned to her. Moments later, she stepped up to the deli counter with her book under one arm and the bouquet clutched in the other, her newfound happiness foreign.

As she searched in her bag for her wallet, a woman walked in. When she saw Sarah, she froze, an inscrutable look in her eyes.

It was Juliette, again. Despite the cold weather, she was wearing a short dress, the kind that emphasized her long, toned legs. Sarah felt her euphoria give way to self-consciousness.

"What—what are you doing here?" she demanded.

"I'm—I was getting flowers for a friend." Juliette looked at her intently. "She lives down the street."

Sarah's mind whirled. Eric was away, or at least she'd thought he was; why did she have to keep running into the woman who was trying to steal him from her? Why couldn't they keep their affair a better secret?

Throwing her money down on the counter, she rushed out of the deli.

* * *

The following morning, in the shower, Sarah stood for a long time letting the water wash over her. She imagined Lawrence, his ocean eyes and deep gaze, his strong hands on her. He'd said she was beautiful. He'd watched her.

She soaped herself all over, imagining Lawrence there with her, watching her now. Her fingers lightly brushed her vagina, lingering there as she remembered their kiss. She didn't touch herself often anymore. Since things had become difficult with

Eric, she found herself thinking of it as shameful and wrong. But today dark liquid heat rushed through every part of her as her fingers moved, Lawrence filling her with a fog of heat, excitement, and lust.

As she was nearing climax, a breeze blew through the bathroom as the door suddenly swung open. She jumped, her heart beating fast.

Eric crossed into the bathroom.

"I've been knocking on the door," he said impatiently. "Why didn't you answer?"

"God, Eric! Really?" she shouted, her arousal chilling instantly to embarrassment. Had he seen her pleasuring herself? "I thought you were away!"

"You didn't answer," he said again. "I was nervous."

Dripping wet, Sarah stepped out of the shower, grabbing a towel and covering her naked body. She felt embarrassed and exposed.

"I'm fine! There's no need to worry about me! What are you doing home, anyway?"

"We have to talk, Sarah." It was his serious, taking-care-of-business voice. Did he know, somehow? She wasn't ready for this now. Ignoring him, she crossed out of the bathroom to the open window and shut it violently.

"I still think it would be good for you to go away for a bit," he said. "Take a break."

She faced him defiantly. "What do you mean, go away?"

"You've been acting strangely again, you know you have. You've been regressing. Are you even taking your medication?"

Could he have seen? No—she'd made sure to throw the other half of the pill away when she'd cut it. "Yes, I'm taking my medication," she snapped. "Not like you'd notice anyway."

His expression softened, a little. "Can you blame me for worrying?"

"Worrying! While you're off doing whatever you want." She looked at him with disgust. "You think I believe that?"

His face hardened. "Don't start this again, Sarah," he said. "We really shouldn't have to go through this every time. You know I have to take these trips. It's my goddamn *job*. It's what keeps us in this beautiful home, our kids in good schools—"

"You know that isn't what I'm talking about," she spat back.

"I can't just stop working to cater to your unreasonable jealousy."

"Unreasonable?" she yelled. "Christ, Eric. I wish you would just be honest with me, just for once."

"I am, Sarah. I can't be any more honest than this with you." He took her hand, his gentleness surprising. She flinched. "Please don't do this," he said. "I thought—I thought the therapy was helping you. I need you to try. Our kids—"

She snatched her hand back from him, the rage flaring up again. "Our kids are conveniently gone, Eric. *You* sent them away. You knew it killed me, and you did it anyway." It felt even more miserable to speak the words out loud. "I can't be their mother anymore, except for on the weekends and long holidays."

"That's not true," he said. "You're as much their mother as you ever were. And we didn't send them to boarding school to hurt you, Sarah. It was for their benefit. They needed—"

"Oh, that's bullshit, Eric! It was to keep them from seeing what's really going on," she seethed. "To keep them from seeing that their father is lying and living a double life. To keep them from coming to their own conclusions about what kind of a man their father really is."

"Sarah, I know you're—"

"You don't know anything!" she shouted, her vehemence surprising her. "You barely know me anymore! Have you ever noticed how I like to dog-ear my books or write in the margins?"

Eric looked at her, confused. "What does that have to do with anything?"

She couldn't hold back the tears any longer. "I'll just go on being this perfect little reflection of what you want me to be, and you—" She looked hard at him, hating him for leaving her so vulnerable.

Eric moved toward her, but she was already running from the room.

* * *

When he was gone, she went through her morning rituals in a distracted daze.

Laura called, and for some reason she answered, trying hard to muster enough cheeriness to put her off. That plan had back-fired, however, and the call had ended with them making plans to get lunch and talk about the event for the museum committee.

Laura was constantly volunteering and planning and... well, *doing* things. She reminded Sarah of herself, once upon a time, the constantly busy, never-sit-still Sarah she'd once prided herself on being. All that activity struck Sarah as tedious these days. Laura was constantly encouraging Sarah to join her, to be "more herself," and, to make matters worse, when Sarah did join her, Laura tended to pick places where other uptown socialites congregated, eyeing each other's designer shoes and comparing Birkin bags.

As soon as she could get away, Sarah found herself once again in the park. She'd seen no sign of Lawrence yet and had no way of knowing how much longer she should wait around.

As if in answer, she heard a deep voice speak to her.

She turned to find Lawrence walking toward her. He pulled her in and kissed her, a long kiss that took her by surprise. This time there was no resistance on her part. She felt her knees go weak as he held her and looked into her eyes.

"Since yesterday, I've been wanting to do that again," he said.

"I'm glad you did," she whispered back.

Sarah nodded. She realized with a stab of guilt that she'd thought of him more over the last evening than she had of her own family.

His hand lightly brushed her breast as he brought it to her waist.

It didn't matter one bit to Sarah who he was or where he came from. She took his hand and let him lead her. They left the playground area and wandered around the park. They walked around the reservoir, where sunlight floated over the water, runners passing them while they walked in silence. The city spread out above the southern end of the lake, noiseless and magical in the distance. Their two hands locked, Lawrence's brushed against Sarah's outer thigh, sending shivers up her spine.

He broke the silence. "It feels like we're somewhere else, doesn't it?"

She looked over the serene water, glittering in the sun. It did indeed feel like that—like somewhere else.

"I don't come here enough...or come here at all, anymore," she said. "I mean, I used to, when—" she thought of her kids, their days in the park together, "when I had a reason to come," she finished quietly.

"I come here a lot," he said. "In a city like this, you need a special place, somewhere that takes you out of your life, where you can hide. This is it for me."

Sarah stopped. "Lawrence," she said. "We need to clear up at least some of this mystery. I don't know anything about you, except that you're well-versed in Zola and you like to talk to strangers."

"Only very beautiful strangers," he said flirtatiously. "And that I write; don't forget about that."

"But you won't let me read anything," Sarah persisted. "You see how this could all seem kind of strange, right?"

His face darkened, and part of her immediately wished she could take it back.

"People get to know each other too well, they lose that magic, the ability to be each other's hiding places. Do we want to give that up?" he asked.

When she didn't respond, he sighed. "All right, fine—I give up," he said, putting his hands up in mock surrender as they walked on. "What do you want to know about me?"

"Everything," Sarah said.

"How about this: you get three questions." He turned to look at her and smiled.

"Only three?"

"Only three. And there are rules."

Sarah smiled, already enjoying the game. "I hate rules."

"One rule, then," he said. "Nothing too specific: names, dates, things like that. I want to preserve at least that little bit of mystery."

"Then, what's the point?"

"You can still ask general stuff. Get creative." He held her by the shoulders, looking deeply into her eyes. "Look," he said, his voice softer. "I'll tell you everything there is to know about me when the time is right."

She felt her cheeks redden, and she averted her eyes. She took a moment to think. "Did you grow up in New York?"

"Yes, I did."

"Do you have siblings?"

"I have an older sister, Beatrice, who lives in Paris. She married a French doctor and has three little monsters, whom I adore."

"That was a good one," Sarah said, enjoying the interrogation.

"We grew up very close to each other, my sister and I," he went on. "Our parents were too busy to take care of us, so we took care of each other." He turned thoughtful for a moment. "See, I'm not completely unfair; I'll throw in a freebie or two." He smiled. "One more question—make it a good one."

It was a long shot, but she figured she might as well try. "What's your last name?"

"Nope! Remember our rules. That's way too specific."

Her eyes searched his. "Have you ever had your heart broken?"

He looked at her intently. "Not yet," he said.

Sarah looked away to contain the heat rising in her chest.

"What makes you want to be so secretive?" she asked.

He wagged a finger at her. "That's four. You only get three."

ENTRY, OCTOBER 25, 2018
Patient: Sarah Rock
Age: 39 (Dob: 12/7/1978)

Sarah was especially upbeat in today's session. Her mood swings are becoming more frequent, which is concerning; though she hasn't mentioned the nightmares again recently.

She has spoken of her new friend, Lawrence, in connection with her newfound sense of purpose but refuses to go into it further than saying they occasionally speak to each other in the park. She mentioned the book that they are both interested in—*Thérèse Raquin*. Lawrence is nothing more than a friend to her, apparently the two of them have not exchanged contact information or much infor-mation at all beyond their first names.

Sarah didn't mention Eric or the kids at all during today's session or her paranoia about Eric's coworker Juliette. It was unusual for her. We ended our session early.

We didn't work with any hypnosis today; I will follow through with it next session. She obviously doesn't trust me as she has in the past; I need her to want to be here before we can do the work that is needed.

# CHAPTER 7

*The two sweethearts from the commencement found their*
*intrigue necessary, inevitable and quite natural.*
**THÉRÈSE RAQUIN**

"Is it ready to taste yet?" Darcy asked.

"Not yet, sweetie," Sarah said. "I've got to add some more tomatoes before it'll be quite right. Just give me a minute."

It was the weekend again. Sarah had picked up their favorite, the Goddess's fried chicken (which, after the requisite alterations, Eric had christened "General Sarah's Chicken"), and was now adding seasoned tomatoes and lemon to complete its transformation into a homemade meal. Her favorite romantic music was playing on the stereo, and she sang along as she chopped. Eric had always hated this kind of music—but who cared? She felt free and light, able to do whatever she wanted: the bright flip side to being ignored by your spouse. How was that for thinking positively?

She wondered whether Dr. Robin had believed her at their session. Had she really accepted her reticence about Lawrence as easily as she'd seemed to? It was impossible to tell with her; sometimes she felt as if the therapist read her mind. But Sarah was hopeful now, something that she hadn't felt in years. She wasn't about to jeopardize that by inviting the kind of judgment she knew Dr. Robin would express. Anyway, one afternoon in the park had done what all those thousands of countless, meaningless hours on the couch hadn't. It had restored her hope.

If only she could find out something, anything, about Lawrence! She sighed, thinking of all the fruitless, furtive work she'd put in. She'd tried searching online for Lawrence—for his name, for his writing, even for his sister in Paris—the man was a ghost, even more of an internet non-entity than Dr. Robin. She just didn't know enough about him. It made things exciting, she had to admit.

A bloodcurdling scream pierced her daydream. Surprised, she slipped with the knife, cutting her finger and drawing blood. She felt a quick jolt of pain and swore to herself as she clutched her finger. Darcy rushed across the kitchen to her side, shaking her own hand violently.

"Mommy!" she sobbed. "I touched the stove."

She held out her hand. The burn was an angry red, already starting to blister. Sarah took hold of her hand and plunged it under cold water, her daughter's winces cutting through her.

"It's okay—it's okay, sweet baby," she repeated gently as she stroked the girl's long hair to soothe her. She took an ice pack out of the freezer and held it to Darcy's hand. "Hold that, honey—it's just a burn, it'll be all right."

As Darcy quieted down, her face changed from upset to alarm. She wiped away her tears abruptly and pointed past her mother.

"Mommy—are *you* all right?" she said.

Sarah looked. On the kitchen counter were a few drops of blood, which continued into an impressive-looking trail.

"Of course," she said, covering her alarm. "It's just a little cut."

She put her cut finger under the faucet, too, then wrapped a paper towel around it to stop the bleeding. She got out a Band-Aid and applied it, watching as the blood soaked quickly through.

Ominous thoughts flitted through her head: Would she be willing to hurt her family for her secret? Pushing the guilty thought away, she drew Darcy into a close hug.

She said in a calm voice, "It's just a little burn. It'll heal up soon—just try to keep it protected for a while, okay? You want to hold onto the ice pack for now?"

Darcy nodded and Sarah felt the guilt return as she looked into her daughter's big, gray-green eyes. They were Eric's eyes, the part of him that had been most obviously passed onto their daughter. It was those eyes that she had fallen so deeply in love with, once upon a time—that vulnerable, soulful look. Sarah felt she could hardly bear the look of them, but then they turned away—Darcy's pain and need for Sarah gone, almost as quickly as it had come.

"I love you, honey," Sarah said, her voice cracking.

"I love you too, Mommy," already on her way to the next thing.

* * *

Sarah was happy to have the kids home for dinner. Jason ate three servings then disappeared into his room, as was his habit these days. Darcy followed soon after. Sarah's mind drifted away to Lawrence again.

Just then, she realized that Eric had arrived and had sat down next to her.

"The kids have already eaten," she said while passing him his plate.

"You look different today," he said.

"How so?" she asked, trying to hide her smile behind her wine glass.

"Happy—you actually seem happy." He was smiling, too. Sarah felt herself blush.

"I am. Does that surprise you?"

He ignored her and said, "I'm going to have to go away again next week, Sarah." A somber look came over his face.

For once, she actually felt relieved. Looking at him as she wiped her mouth, she called to the kids. "Who wants dessert?"

"Me," came Darcy's response.

She pushed her chair back and got up. "I'll be in with it in a minute," Sarah called back.

Eric watched as she got out the ice cream, his face puzzled.

He leaned in. "Sarah," he whispered, "I know we said we would go to the country house on Thursday. But I can't change this. I have to go. You know that."

"It's fine," she said. "I'll go on my own." She took out a bowl, put it down on the counter. "It's not like I wasn't expecting to anyway."

"Please, Sarah," he pleaded.

She hissed. "What do you want from me, Eric? The kids are going to be gone through next weekend—and now you're gone this week, too? We're losing our grip on the life we've made together."

She heard Darcy call out to her from the other room, her voice uncertain.

"Mom?"

"Coming, sweetie," she called back. Without looking at him, she went on. "Eric, I don't want to talk about this now. I'm enjoying having them here, and I don't want to think about how you're never here. Is that so complicated?" She stabbed at the ice cream furiously. "You've got to be gone again, fine. I'm going to the country house alone. The tree needs to be taken care of after the storm, along with a lot of other things. We have a life, Eric, if you don't remember."

Eric shook his head. "I don't like you going there alone, Sarah. You're not—" He stopped himself.

She turned on him. "I'm not what, Eric? Go ahead, say it!"

"Stable," Eric said defiantly.

Sarah scoffed. "How *dare* you lecture me about stability, Eric? Do you really think walking out on your family for a young girl is acting *stable*?"

"Please Sarah," he said.

"Do you?"

"Stop!" he demanded.

"At least I'm *here*." She picked up the bowl of ice cream. "You want to be gone all the time, I don't need you lecturing me whenever you're here. Now if you'll excuse me, I'm going to bring this out to our daughter."

She stormed out of the room before he could answer.

\* \* \*

It wasn't until Monday that she was able to get away to her park bench again.

Sunday night had been restless, and even after her morning cup of coffee she still felt fuzzy. The kids had needed seeing off much earlier than she'd been ready to get up; it felt like the medication was still making her groggy.

*Thérèse Raquin* lay like a lead weight across her leg. She looked at the book, aware that she wouldn't be able to concentrate on it if she read it now. The novel was intense and surprisingly close to home; she found herself sympathizing with its heroine even while she recoiled from her craziness. There was something victim-like about her, despite the cold calculation it took to plot her husband's murder; her insanity was a condition thrust upon her, a result of her having been abandoned throughout her life.

She sat on the bench for a while, trying not to let her thoughts veer too much in this morose direction. Then a familiar shape caught her attention, and she saw Lawrence entering the park at a brisk stride, strolling toward her with a big smile on his face. He was wearing soft blue jeans and his gray jacket. She felt the joy spread across her face in response and hoped he wouldn't notice how giddy she was. She stood to meet him.

A voice came from behind her, cutting through her school-girl excitement.

"Sarah! *Sarah!*"

She turned quickly, her face sinking.

It was Laura, walking toward her with long strides. The familiar cheery smile was nowhere in sight. Sarah glanced back in the other direction; Lawrence had already turned and walked

THE WOMAN IN THE PARK

discreetly off to one side of the path. How had he managed to do that so smoothly?

"Sarah," Laura said, annoyance barely detectable in her voice. "What's going on with you?"

Had she seen Lawrence? "What—what do you mean, what's going on with me?"

"We had lunch plans," Laura said. "Remember, to go over the event? I tried calling you."

"I'm so sorry, Laura, I've just been so distracted lately," Sarah apologized. She looked past her friend for Lawrence, but he'd disappeared.

"Are you sure that's it?" Laura said, following her gaze. She looked at Sarah again, her eyes narrowing.

"I've just been really busy lately. We're renovating the country house; we had that tree we planted, as a family. The storm hit it hard, and—" She felt herself babbling and reined it in. "The kids are away this weekend, so I'm going up there on Thursday for a few days, just to tidy some things up. Look at the tree, that kind of thing. Can we plan on doing lunch sometime before that? I'm sorry, I'll be there this time. I promise."

Laura didn't look convinced.

"You know I would do anything for you, right?" she said abruptly.

Sarah's embarrassment turned to annoyance. Why did everyone want to take care of her? She swallowed the frustration back. "I know, Laura. Believe me, I do."

Laura's face brightened. "What if I came with you to the country house. You know I love it up there with all those quaint little shops; we could make a day trip out of it! I could help you with some of the things that need doing, and we could go antiquing. What do you think?"

"I just think I need to get up there on my own, think some things through. I'll be around for lunch beforehand if you want."

"If you're sure. I'll look at my schedule."

Sarah nodded.

"I'll call you later?"

They cheek-kissed goodbye, and Laura sped off down the path.

When she was gone, Sarah looked around for Lawrence again. Evidently her friend had spooked him; he'd vanished.

## CHAPTER 8

*When Laurent parted from her, after his initial visit, he staggered like a drunken man, and the next day, on recovering his cunning prudent calm, he asked himself whether he should return to this young woman whose kisses gave him the fever. First of all he positively decided to keep to himself. Then he had a cowardly feeling. He sought to forget, to avoid seeing Thérèse, and yet she always seemed to be there, implacably extending her arms. The physical suffering that this spectacle caused him became intolerable.*

**THÉRÈSE RAQUIN**

The stark, white walls of Dr. Robin's office seemed to be leaning in on her. Her own skin felt wrong, too tight. Something felt wrong about the air, too; it was thick, unmoving, the air inside a parked car on a hot day.

"Can we open a window?" Sarah asked, already up and moving towards it. "It's stifling in here."

"Of course, go right ahead," Dr. Robin answered. "Get yourself comfortable, however you'd like. Let me get you a glass of water, too. Is everything all right?"

Sarah squirmed, her high heels chafing her feet. "It's just really hot in here. You don't feel it?"

"I'm afraid I don't." Dr. Robin poured water from a ceramic pitcher into a glass and handed it to her. She drank it all in one gulp, feeling momentary relief as the cool water spread down her throat. Dr. Robin looked at her, concerned.

"How about we try to breathe a moment, just to get ourselves centered," she suggested.

"All right," Sarah said, closing her eyes.

"Let's count from ten, backwards." Dr. Robin's voice was soft, peaceful. "Start with ten, nine, eight—"

"Seven, six, five," Sarah continued. An image of Eric and Juliette flashed across her mind, and she faltered.

"Breathe deeply," Dr. Robin continued.

She thought of Lawrence, of his particular smell.

"Four, three…two, one."

When she opened her eyes, the therapist was looking at her with the same concerned expression.

"What's been going on, Sarah?" she asked. "You seemed so happy last week, so upbeat. I can't help but notice that you seem particularly anxious today. Has something happened in the meantime that you want to talk about?"

She didn't want to talk about it. She wanted to stand up and run out the door, out of the room, out of her life. Just go, without stopping or looking back.

Instead she leaned back in the couch, the change of posture doing nothing to relax her.

"I don't know. I really don't," she said. Lawrence came into her head again, and she shook her head violently to clear him from her thoughts. "I just feel so empty all the time. Like I'm just here, empty—waiting for something to come along."

"Do you have any sense about what you're waiting for?" Dr.

Robin asked, her calm self-possession infuriating. "What about the woman in the park? Has seeing her with her children upset you again?"

Sarah thought about that for a minute and then shook her head and said, "No it's not about that."

Sarah looked out the window to keep her face from giving her away. She couldn't bear the therapist's stare right now, couldn't bear her questioning. How was it that she was already so close to the truth?

"I lost touch with a friend," she said. "A good friend."

"Which friend?" Dr. Robin asked.

"It doesn't matter." Sarah looked out the window again. Outside, a woman and a man were arguing over something. Their voices fell into a staccato rhythm as they interrupted each other.

"It matters, Sarah." Dr. Robin placed her journal beside her. "You remember what we've said about the truth here? As long as it's true, it matters—and this is a safe place to say it. It may not seem like it matters right away, but the truth is always where we have to start. Something tells me this is more than a friendship gone awry. It's something more important than that, something closer to you. Is it the man you met? The one from the park?" She picked up her journal again, flipped to a page. "Lawrence?"

It was useless trying to lie to her. Sarah nodded.

"That's not an insignificant thing at all," the doctor went on. "You seemed very excited to have met him. You found a connection with him, isn't that right?"

Sarah nodded again. The man outside had stormed away from the woman, and she stood looking after him, shaking her head.

"I don't even know him," Sarah said. "It's ridiculous."

"It's not ridiculous," Dr. Robin assured her again. "Did you disagree about something? Fight about something?"

"Not even. I just haven't seen him in a few days, and I was worried, that's all."

"Worried that you'd offended him somehow?"

*Or that he's just come to his senses and changed his mind,* she thought. "I haven't exactly had a chance to offend him."

"What are you worried about?"

How could she say it without sounding like a fool? "I don't know," she said. "Maybe just that something bad happened to him."

The therapist jotted something down. "What would make you think that?"

"I don't know, what makes anyone think it?" Sarah frowned. "Bad things happen all the time, don't they?"

"They do," the therapist agreed. "But couldn't he just be busy? Didn't you say he was an editor?"

"A writer."

"A busy profession, or at least it can be." Dr. Robin leaned in with the air of someone about to change the subject. "Perhaps it would be worthwhile for us to explore why not seeing him has you so anxious."

"What do you mean?" Sarah asked, on guard.

"Given your abandonment issues—your husband, your children away at school, the loss of your parents when you were young—don't you think this might be getting to you in some special way that we might want to talk about?"

Sarah looked around the room and sat in silence.

The therapist smiled. "Are you planning on looking for him

in the park after our session today?"

"Maybe," Sarah admitted.

"You said before that you hadn't exchanged any contact information with Lawrence, or last names. Is that still the case?"

Sarah coughed, embarrassed. "Yeah, it is."

"Do you just wait in the same spot for him at the park each time? I know that routines are important to you," Dr. Robin stated.

"Maybe too important." Sarah laughed, a small dry sound. "He's probably just been busy, like you say."

"I'm sure he's fine," the doctor said, her smile reassuring.

"And I don't really know anything about him," Sarah went on.

"Let's get into that," Dr. Robin said. "That seems to be a good place to start."

* * *

When Sarah emerged, the day was gray, dark clouds covering the sky. She went to the park anyway; she needed to see him. She waited a while on the bench, alone. Distant rain threatened, but she hardly took notice. The magic she had felt there earlier seemed flushed away with the fallen leaves and autumn rain.

A rustle woke her from her daze. She felt a flutter, then the rustle again: a faint, scraping sound, very near her. It was coming from under her bench. She looked down under her legs. There was a bird there, its body twisted and hurt. It tried in vain to flap its wings then paused, its panicked eyes meeting hers.

She bent down and stroked the bird's wing. The bird shuddered away from her, flapping its wings again. Yet its movements were feebler now; it was dying. She held her hands gently around the bird to calm it; in her grasp, it gave out its last breath.

She felt the oppression of loss, the cruel relentlessness of life and death. The rain began to fall. She had to go.

The rain turned quickly to a downpour. Through it she saw a man walking toward her and stood up straight, light again inside. He walked closer—then continued by her without stopping. It wasn't him.

* * *

In the lobby of her building, she met Manuel, who took her drenched coat and shook it off. Too depressed even to respond to his cheerful banter, she got in the elevator and leaned heavily against the side, spent. The door began to close behind her.

The door jolted open, stopped by a reaching arm. She could feel him right away—practically smell him—and then Lawrence stepped past the doors and into the elevator. A burst of fear ran through her, accompanied by excitement.

Without a word, Lawrence kissed her while the doors closed. Sarah's hesitation fled at his touch. As his tongue found hers, her anger dissipated, and she felt again that she was his. She felt excitement run through her body, hot within the chill of their wet clothes; she had to have him. The days she'd spent without him forgotten in the rush of reunion.

The elevator doors opened, and Sarah guided Lawrence to her door, fumbling for her keys. Thank God Eric was away. He couldn't keep his hands off of her. Reluctantly she pulled away, catching her breath.

"Where were you?" she whispered.

"I'm sorry," he whispered back. "I needed time. I won't leave again, Sarah—not unless you want me to." He hesitated at the door.

"I don't want you to," she admitted. Her eyes went to the door, then found his again.

They were inside in a moment, kissing again as she kicked the door shut behind them. She unbuttoned his wet shirt as his hands sought out the edges of her own soaking clothes. She thought she'd never experienced such intensity before. She didn't even care how he had found out where she lived. None of it mattered to her. She was just thrilled to see him.

She looked deeply into his mesmerizing eyes, caressed his strong chest. He pulled off the last of her clothes and stood looking at her. To her amazement she wasn't ashamed of her less-than-perfect body and its softness, or her age. In his gaze, she knew she was beautiful. She also knew there was no turning back from this moment; she would be an adulteress, a thing she had despised and vilified. But in that gaze, even that was transformed: in that gaze, she knew she no longer cared.

He slowly pulled down her panties and kissed her between her legs. She moaned softly as he licked faster, exploring her with his hands and mouth. He stood up and looked her in the eyes, then pushed her against the wall, kissing her all over. He took her firm nipples into his mouth and devoured them; after a moment they slid to the floor together, unable to wait any longer. He slowly pressed into her, and she moaned softly, relishing each thrust. Her thoughts of guilt and loss were forgotten. She let her body go, surrendering to his touch, and they moved as one until they came together in a climax that felt as though it shook her every cell.

Afterward, they made their way to her bed, tracing one another's bodies with their hands. It was jarring to have a different man's body occupying it, a different man's face; Lawrence was bigger than Eric, but his face was softer and more round. She lay for a while, looking into his smoky blue eyes before she spoke.

"I've never done this before," she said quietly.

She realized she wanted him again. Was this what obsession felt like? She was afraid, startled by the intensity of her own feeling.

"What is it?" he asked, as though reading her mind.

"Nothing," she said, furrowing her brow. "It's just that—now you know me. The mystery's over, at least part of it." She smiled apologetically at him.

He didn't answer.

"That's my husband," she said, gesturing to a photo on the nightstand beside them of Eric and her, on their wedding day. She realized—could it be, for the first time?—that she wasn't smiling in it.

Lawrence reached past the wedding photo for another one of Sarah with her children, all smiling. The kids were smaller then; it was how she often thought of them.

"Beautiful family," he said.

"Yeah," she said sadly. Jason hardly resembled that little boy anymore, with his soft eyes and open face. "They're in boarding school," she added, her tone oddly accusatory.

"Do you miss them? I'm sorry, stupid question. Of course, you must. Why are they there?" Lawrence stroked her cheek gently.

She sighed. "I guess Eric wanted them to have a normal life."

"What exactly does that mean?" he inquired.

She hesitated. Would it be telling him too much? "I suppose I've been a bit—well, depressed and out of sorts, the past few years. He—Eric—he wanted them to be away from that for a while."

"Depressed? Why?"

"I don't really know why. I mean, sometimes I think I do, but I don't."

"The triad of depression," he said softly.

"What's that?"

"'I'm not good enough, this world is a miserable place, the future is hopeless.' Negative thoughts become vicious cycles."

"That sounds familiar," she said. So they knew that about each other, too.

"We have to let go of those thoughts," he said. "It's a choice, living in the moment. No one's ever fully happy. That's a myth we all subscribe to."

"I know. It's just… I feel like—I'm underwater and gasping for air, only the air never comes." She smiled back at him, into his clear eyes. "I'm not sad now."

Lawrence pulled her in and kissed her. "That's good," he said in a husky voice, kissing her again. "That means I serve a purpose."

"I guess you do," she breathed, giddy again. A wild idea occurred to her: the country house.

He reached across her to place the photo back on the nightstand, face down.

Together they fell back into the cloud of sheets, the darkness of the room hiding them.

ENTRY, OCTOBER 30, 2018
Patient: Sarah Rock
Age: 39 (Dob: 12/7/1978)

Sarah was extremely agitated today. She seemed dehydrated and tired, as if she hasn't been sleeping properly. She also continues to lie to me, sometimes transparently. But we broke through a little today. She mentioned feeling helpless, even lost, in her daily routine. She briefly reminisced about Halloween with her children and wished she were spending it again with them this year.

Otherwise, it seems she is transferring her familial concerns to her friend from the park, Lawrence. She insists she is taking her medications as directed, though she is showing signs of having tapered off the antidepressant, though pharmacist confirms that she has been picking up her prescriptions.

# CHAPTER 9

*But at the present moment, face to face with their anxious
expectation and timorous desires, they felt the imperative
necessity of closing their eyes, and of dreaming of a future
full of amorous felicity and peaceful enjoyment.*
THÉRÈSE RAQUIN

Lunch with Laura the following day was on her schedule.

It was amazing how much of a difference seeing Lawrence
made, and not simply in the ways she would have expected.
As much as she'd wanted to avoid getting together with Laura
before, now the added secret made their meeting almost deliri-
ously exciting. She found it a wonderful new thrill to keep so
vast a secret from her friend; Laura's natural inquisitiveness
only made it that much more of a challenge, as though getting
through an interview with her might somehow prepare Sarah
for the more daunting task of concealing the affair from her
husband and her therapist.

She wanted to find out, too, whether her friend had seen Lawrence in the park the other day; she knew Laura would never be so tactless as to come out and say such a thing directly. That she had ended her last meeting with Lawrence by inviting him up to the country house with her on Thursday—exactly the invitation she had denied her friend—only made the secret that much richer.

Sarah arrived at the restaurant beating the always-early Laura to the table. The little Pont Neuf Bistro was crowded as it often was on afternoons, full of Carnegie Hill regulars and older folks there for a little light French cuisine.

Laura arrived perfectly put-together as usual, decked out in high boots and a gorgeous new autumn coat, a form-fitting white number with a thick fur collar and a tight belt. It made a marked contrast to the turtleneck and wide yellow scarf Sarah had thrown on, on her way out the door; yet despite Laura's picture-perfect Upper East Side look, for once Sarah felt no desire to compete with her. She knew her secret had put her into a different ball game altogether.

They settled in and ordered seared tuna and frisée salad with mustard vinaigrette. The waiter's accent was thick enough to be fake, and Sarah wondered if he was actually an actor refining his craft among the easygoing patrons. *So much falsehood everywhere,* she thought, tickled to be adding to that sea of deception.

The two friends' conversation flowed easily. It wasn't hard for Sarah to concentrate on the topics at hand; her mission to conceal her affair from Laura made her genuinely eager to talk about whatever Laura wanted. For an hour they gossiped, planned, and scheduled in the offhand way they'd once been accustomed to, Laura seemingly all too happy to have her old

Sarah back. Even the superficiality of their high-society doings felt fitting to Sarah—in hiding something behind them, it was as if she was finally able to use them for their real purpose.

Near the end of their meal, after a deadly serious digression into floral centerpieces, silent-auction items, and vegan food choices, Laura leaned in and squeezed her arm affectionately.

"I'm happy we did this," she said, nodding meaningfully.

"Me too," Sarah answered. She realized she almost meant it. "I felt so badly the other day when we ran into each other."

"There was nothing to feel badly about," Laura reassured her. "I was just worried about you. I probably pushed too hard."

Sarah searched her friend's face for signs of reticence but saw nothing. Perhaps Laura hadn't spotted Lawrence.

After they'd finished their too-strong espresso coffees and the too-small French chocolates that came with them, they paid and walked out of the restaurant. Laura leaned in to kiss her cheek goodbye.

"Let's make sure to do it again," Laura said. "Have fun upstate!"

She hurried off down Madison Avenue, leaving Sarah to wonder just how much that Upper East Side smile concealed.

\* \* \*

Thursday could not come quickly enough.

Inviting Lawrence to the country house with her had lent the trip a delicious anticipation. With Eric and the kids away, it was hard to concentrate on much else. She had her hair and nails done, waxed every hair from her body, skipped her morning pills. She couldn't have them fogging her senses—not now. Only the call to Dr. Robin to reschedule gave her anxiety, and in the end she simply decided not to show up. Paying for the missed session was worth not having to come up with excuses.

She picked Lawrence up by the park, realizing yet again that she had no idea where he lived. A part of her didn't want to know. He had been right; the mystery was tantalizing and enhanced the magic between them.

They left the city, and the roads became less crowded. They turned onto a winding country road where the trees had lost most of their leaves, the barren limbs showing an expansive sky ahead—autumn sun slanting through the trees, a mellow strobe across the pavement.

She was wearing a skirt, and he rubbed her bare leg as she drove, his fingers slowing as he moved his hand up from her knee. She quivered at his touch as his hand moved further, slowly creeping up her skirt. With a mischievous look he began to caress her, back and forth, and she moaned as she felt herself becoming wet under his touch.

"Stop, please," she said, the car swerving a bit. Did she mean it? It felt dangerous, but she didn't want to stop him. If anything, she wanted him underneath her, inside her. But they were moving fast, there was traffic around them—

"Stop," she whispered again.

"I don't think you really want me to stop," he teased. He continued to touch her, pushing his fingers deeper this time.

She moaned again, gripping the steering wheel to steady the car. A pickup truck blared its horn as it passed.

The road was almost empty now. She took the opportunity to slow down and pulled over to the side of the road as he kept going, faster, and she gave in completely.

She opened her eyes, panting. He was looking at her, that

mischievous smile still on his face. Reaching across for her, he gently pulled her up over the console and onto him, the heat from their breath already fogging up the windows.

* * *

They drove again for some time before she stopped the car in front of an old hardware store called McNally's. It had been there for decades, maybe even a century: a grandfather-father-son shop with lots of character. Sarah had visited it many times. Together they walked up the gravel path, lined with forest green bushes, to the entrance.

Inside, they were met by the stale smell of tools and cigar smoke. Sarah hated cigar and cigarette smoke in general; the smell was putrid to her, reminding her of dead things. Her father sometimes smoked a cigar.

"Do you smoke?" she asked Lawrence impulsively.

Lawrence shook his head, and she was relieved.

Two clerks stood in the front of the store, chatting with customers. Sarah walked toward the back of the store to the gardening section and picked out a couple of pruning tools from a shelf. She'd probably have to replant the tree altogether, but it was worth seeing whether any part of it could be saved.

On her way back she found Lawrence looking at a collection of vintage Swiss Army knives. He was studying one, turning it over in his hands.

"My father had a knife collection when I was a kid," he said, faraway in thought.

"Another teeny tiny bit of information," she teased, coming in close. "Does he still collect them?"

Lawrence's face turned somber. "No, he doesn't," he said, his voice a bit harder. "He died."

Sarah felt terrible. "I'm sorry," she said.

He replaced the knife. "It's all right. I don't know what happened to them. The knives, I mean. My mother took them, gave them away, I think. I always loved them."

He walked off to the front of the store, deep in thought.

When he was gone, Sarah took the knife back off the shelf and brought it up to the clerk to buy it along with the rest of her tools. She found Lawrence outside, waiting by the car.

"My gift to you," she said, tapping him with the knife. To her surprise, he kept his face averted, clearly deep in thought. "I'm sorry," she said softly. "I thought it would make you happy."

Lawrence turned to her, pain in his eyes. He took the knife and smiled wistfully at it.

"He was an okay dad, I guess, but fine. My mother, though she was never the same." He said quietly and took a deep breath. "I'm sorry, I do appreciate that you got that for me. It's been a long time; I don't know why it sometimes hits me like it does."

"You were just a kid. I understand." She swallowed hard. "I lost my parents when I was young, too. They died together in an accident." She felt the awkwardness it always brought up when she said it, as though she was talking about someone else's life. "My grandparents raised me."

"God, I'm so sorry." His voice had softened again.

"It's all right," she said. "They were good parents. And I've had a long time to get used to it."

He drew her in for an embrace. She felt safe for the first time in a long while.

* * *

At last they arrived at the country house, a stately white Victorian with big windows and a garden with tall trees and bushes. The house was well kept, the grounds immaculate—except for the old oak tree right beside the house, which conspicuously needed care. Out of place with the harmony all around, it was missing several branches, had a dark spot down the center, and looked as though it were dead.

Lawrence eyed the tree thoughtfully as they parked the car, and Sarah thought he might say something about it when they got out. But he didn't mention it.

"This place is beautiful," he exclaimed instead, looking around.

"I used to love coming here every weekend when the kids were little," Sarah sighed, breathing in the country air. "It was our home away from home."

"And now?" he asked.

"Everyone's been too busy to come up."

They went inside. The air was a bit stuffy, dust motes floating around in the sunlight.

"Give me a hand," Sarah said, unlocking one of the windows. "These are old windows—they tend to stick."

They tugged the window up together. A refreshing, cool breeze blew through, and the house felt like a home again.

They headed into the kitchen. Sarah remembered a visit a few years before when she and Eric had spontaneously danced together through the kitchen while dinner was cooking. The kids had sat close by, squinting and shouting in exaggerated embarrassment. Deep down she knew they'd liked it; it had felt good for them all to be together. What had taken that away from them?

They unloaded the car, bringing bags of food into the kitchen. Sarah brought out cheese sandwiches and tomato salad to eat at the kitchen table, and they sat down to eat.

"It feels so comfortable here," Lawrence said breaking the silence.

"Maybe this could be a place for you to write."

A loud bang interrupted them.

Lawrence went out through the garden door to see where the noise came from. There was a bird on the ground flapping around, it had hit their window. He touched the tiny bird. It was now very, very still. Sarah stood silent as Lawrence picked up the bird and brought it to the tree, where he laid it gently on the ground on the other side of its trunk. Together they looked at the bird, motionless on the ground.

\* \* \*

Inside, they cleaned up after lunch while music played in the next room, its cheery noise oblivious to the small tragedy that had just taken place.

"It was sad—that poor bird was so helpless," Sarah said. She brought two cups of coffee to the table and sat down again.

He noticed the book he had bought her peeking out of her bag.

"Did you finish it?" he asked.

"Not yet, I almost don't want to ruin it because I know it won't end well," she replied.

"The beginning is always beautiful," he reflected. "When the lovers meet, they're taken with their passion, and it grows and grows until something…well, sometimes they are driven to madness."

"Do you think we will be?" she asked, her smile uncertain.

"It sounds terrible but, somehow, being crazy in love seems to be what everyone wants."

She looked at him and realized that what he was saying might actually be true.

ENTRY, NOVEMBER 1, 2018
Patient: Sarah Rock
Age: 39 (Dob: 12/7/1978)

Sarah did not attend this week's session or call to reschedule. This is her first no-show in over six months. I've called her repeatedly, but she's not answering. I'll give her space and allow her to make the next appointment when she's ready.

If she doesn't, I'll have to contact someone about her; if she is tapering her medications on her own, the side effects could be more than problematic. At this juncture I do not see her as posing a threat to herself or to anyone else, but her behavior has been erratic and will be worth discussing with her under some neutral pretext.

## CHAPTER 10

*The only ambition of this great powerful frame was to do nothing, to grovel in idleness and satiation from hour to hour. He wanted to eat well, sleep well, to abundantly satisfy his passions, without moving from his place, without running the risk of the slightest fatigue.*

THÉRÈSE RAQUIN

Tap, tap, tap.

She opened her eyes. Moonlight entered through the garden window, filling the room with a soft glow.

*Tap, tap, tap.*

It was coming from outside, a tree branch tapping against the bedroom window. She got up and walked over to it, looked outside into the darkness at the old damaged tree. She felt as if someone was watching them.

Surely Eric hadn't followed them?

She watched for a while, longer than was at all reasonable, before sleep beckoned her back again.

\* \* \*

She woke late, buried deep in the warm covers. Soft sunlight was seeping in from the window. What time was it?

She heard Lawrence's voice: muffled, faraway. It was coming from the bathroom; he was on the phone. It sounded like he was arguing with whoever was on the other end; she could hear him alternately pleading, remonstrating.

"What? No." His voice was strained. "Please, it's too—"

She couldn't make out the rest. She realized that the water was running. Did he have the shower on?

The answer hit her like a splash of cold water and the fog of sleep finally evaporated from her mind. He didn't want her to hear him.

He was married. It was his wife.

She got up from bed, wrapping her robe around her against the morning cold. His gray woolen jacket lay draped over a club chair in the corner. She looked at it, then back at the door. Behind the bathroom door, the heated conversation continued.

She crossed the room to the chair, grabbed the jacket and felt the pockets. She found the pocketknife she'd bought him; nothing else. His voice stopped abruptly, and she scrambled to put the jacket back, draping it carefully across the back of the chair. As she did, something small and hard fell out and rolled across the hardwood floor. She picked it up.

It was a ring.

She felt the coldness of it in her hand, its weight as it clinked softly against her own wedding ring. She looked closely; an inscription ran around the inside, engraved in fine cursive letters.

*B&H—Amor vincit omnia.*

"What are you doing?"

Startled, Sarah stuffed the ring into the pocket of her robe and swung around. Lawrence emerged from the bathroom, phone in hand.

"I was going to ask you that," she said bluntly, her voice louder than she'd intended. Who the hell were B and H? "You were pretty loud on the phone just now; you woke me up."

"That was my editor," he said, clearly annoyed. "He wants me to submit something to him, but I'm not ready to send it yet."

"Seemed like it was more than that," she said.

"No, that's all it was."

She frowned. "You really sounded—"

"Drop it, Sarah." His tone was hostile. "I said that's all it was, and I mean it."

She pulled back from him, alarmed at the turn his voice had taken.

*B&H.*

Had she really wanted this so badly that she'd allowed him to lie to her up to now?

His face softened again. "I'm sorry," he said. "It's just— sometimes there's so much pressure."

She wasn't giving in again. "I understand that. But that wasn't your editor, Lawrence. We need to talk about this."

"About what?"

"Give me your hand."

She took the hand he offered, held up his ring finger. There was the slightest pale band of skin where a ring should be. She felt the rush of vindication—and relief.

"Plain to see," she said. "You're marked."

He looked down, his face dark.

"Now you don't have to tell me her name, but I want to hear

about her. It's only fair."

Lawrence took a deep breath. "I'd rather not," he said.

She stood firm. "You've been to my home, seen photos of my family—slept in *two* of my beds," she said. "You need to tell me something. Is she anything like me, for instance?"

Lawrence looked at her for a long moment. "She's nothing like you," he said finally. "She's frivolous and uninteresting. She doesn't have your depth." When she refused to take that bait, he went on. "We met in college. Her family treated her like a princess, so I got into the habit of doing it, too. She was shiny and pretty and smart but without any scars or chaos to her. No depth. We got married young, in our senior year of college. Her family wanted us to. And it was just—we were so different. She cares about things that have no meaning to me." He stared out the window.

"So why not split up with her?" she challenged him.

"Why haven't you?" he smiled faintly.

She couldn't answer that.

"I've never cheated on her before this," Lawrence went on.

"What did you tell her about where you are now?" she pressed.

"I told her I'm doing research for my novel. Which is true, in a way. I needed space to work—it was just mental space."

An image of Eric flashed through her mind, placing folded shirts in his suitcase. "You told her you were going on a work trip," she said quietly.

He nodded. "It's all that really makes sense to her anyway."

She thrust her hands into the pockets of her robe, feeling his ring there. He'd been right: it was easier when they knew less about each other. Was he B or H? *Thérèse Raquin* popped into her mind, and she laughed, surprised by the thought.

"What?" he asked.

"I just realized something."

"What's that?"

"Your name is Lawrence."

His smile was confused. "You just realized that?"

"Laurent. Thérèse's lover in the novel is Laurent."

He laughed, relieved to change the subject. "I guess it is. I never really thought of it."

His phone beeped, and he ignored it. Sarah couldn't help but wonder if it was his wife.

* * *

While he was getting dressed, she replaced the ring in his jacket pocket, its weight a burden lifted from her.

*Amor vincit omnia*: the strange words rang in her head. She made a mental note to look them up later.

Over coffee she handed Lawrence an extra set of house keys.

"I'm going to visit Jason at school today," she said. "It's not too far from here. They're doing a Parents' Day for the older kids; Darcy's on an overnight trip, but I thought I'd surprise him."

"That's a good idea."

"I think you'll love the town—it's quaint and close enough to walk to. There are some cool antique shops. A good bookstore, too. Maybe we can meet back here for lunch?"

Lawrence smiled. "I'll go to the market, then. I'll make you something fancy. Fondue, maybe. You like fondue?"

"Of course," she said, smiling. She remembered the first time she'd tried it, on a trip to Switzerland with Eric and the kids. It felt like a lifetime ago.

"Fondue it is," Lawrence said.

"He's a good lay, a good cook—is there anything this guy can't do?" she joked.

"The cooking is from summers with my sister in France," he explained. "She taught me everything I know."

She looked into his blue eyes. Couldn't they go back to knowing only minor details about one another?

"*'Two roads diverged in a yellow wood,'*" he said abruptly. "*'And sorry I could not travel both.'*"

Sarah knew she'd heard the lines before. "What's that from?" she asked.

"Robert Frost," he said. "'The Road Not Taken.' It's one of my favorite poems. '*Two roads diverged in a wood, and I—I took the one less traveled by—*'"

"Like the road you're on with me?"

"' *And that has made all the difference,*'" he finished. He took her by the hands. "This is our road, Sarah. We may be meant to be here, right now. We owe it to ourselves, and to them, to find out for sure."

"And if we're wrong?" She searched his eyes. Was he B or H? She questioned to herself.

Did it really matter who he was?

"'*And both that morning equally lay. In leaves no step had trodden black,*'" he quoted again. "Maybe neither path is really wrong—we just think that one of them must be."

"And because we're us, we assume it's the one we're on?" she asked.

He drew her close.

"That's right," he said. "And that's a choice, too."

105

# CHAPTER 11

*After a time, she believed in the reality of this comedy...*
THÉRÈSE RAQUIN

The Cole Manor School occupied a stately green campus a little way upstate, nestled between an impoverished old Hudson River village and an up-and-coming town that attracted hipsters from New York and Boston on the weekends. Wild woods stretched out behind the old red brick buildings; in the distance, the high steeple of a church rose above the foliage.

Sarah parked the car and walked the brick-lined path down to the center of campus. It really was more beautiful than she remembered. On earlier visits to the school with Eric, the place had struck her as impossibly pretentious, an elite prep school where the almost-one-hundred-percent-white student body rowed crew, fenced, and learned to ride horses after classes in (as the school's website boasted) "high-tech science and vector calculus." Ordinarily, privilege never embarrassed Sarah, but here it was hard to escape the awkwardness of it; there was something sad about all these kids being sequestered in the woods from the reality in which their well-off parents toiled back in the city. But today the long green lawns of the campus, its benches and little tables, seemed inviting and harmonious. Farther away down the hill, she could see the river, a placid mirror silently traversed by rowboats. Along its banks, the trees were on fire with vibrant red, orange, and yellow. It was a peaceful place, the very picture of safe, healthy, nurturing.

She stood in front of the tall glass façade of the school library and waited for Jason to appear. The buildings of the campus were inspiring, venerable; for the first time, she found herself wishing she'd been a student here herself. The school housed over 500 children—many of them there because it had proven too burdensome to their parents to keep them at home. Parenting was difficult even for the wealthy; children were a mystery even to the powerful. She looked at the students and parents going in and out of buildings.

She had waited for Jason when he was born, too. He had come late on a hot summer day. At the time her little boy had existed in her mind for so long, she almost couldn't believe he was going to emerge into reality; his little kicks against her stomach, his sleeping and waking twists and turns inside her, had brought out a love that she couldn't imagine attaching to a person. She had loved his being, his life, far more than her own. And when he finally came, she thought she had discovered peace in that ultimate selflessness.

But he was his own person and, with his independence, new fears had awoken in her. Before becoming a mother she'd only had herself to worry about, to care for, to consider in that intimate, unconditional way. Now, having first found unconditional love in another person, she had found unconditional fear too: the constant awareness of her powerlessness to protect and control the life she loved so much. The darkness had returned to her then, more deep-seated than ever, a darkness she felt would take more than a lifetime to let go.

Then she saw him, her Jason, walking across the lawn. He was looking straight ahead, though not at her: an unselfconscious smile on his face. He looked almost as she remembered him: innocent, engaged, open to the world and to life.

She wanted to call out to him and wave, and almost did— and then she saw him laugh to someone else close by. As Sarah watched, a girl stepped forward from one of the library steps to hug Jason. The girl had long dark hair and an olive green jacket; her smile was as open as Jason's. A thought of Juliette flashed through Sarah's mind and she recoiled from it, shocked.

She sat down on the bench nearest her, watching the two children as they laughed and chatted. She couldn't remember when she'd seen her son looking so happy, and the unbidden image of Juliette returned to her mind. Was he this way all the time when away from home?

Was Sarah being replaced for *him*, too?

Then, the girl was up and gone. Jason stood to go too, and when he did, he turned in Sarah's direction. Their eyes met, and for a terrible instant he looked stunned, horrified. Then he came toward her uncertainly, his expression dissolving into vague annoyance.

"What are you doing here, Mom?" he asked in a low voice.

"I'm here to check on the tree and sort some other stuff out, up at the country house," she said. "I thought I'd stop by for Parents' Day." She reached for his hand and gave it a squeeze.

Jason looked at her as if she were speaking a different language.

"The tree?" he asked incredulously. "Mom, you—" He looked around in exasperation. "You shouldn't be here."

She was taken aback. "What do you mean?"

"I'm trying to move on. Don't you get that? You're making it really hard for me."

"Move on?" she repeated, puzzled. "I don't understand. Why is it an issue if I want to see my son?"

"Because *I* don't want to see *you*, Mom. I want to be normal up here. I see you on most weekends. Isn't that enough?"

She was shocked. Teenage rebelliousness was nothing in comparison to this; did he really hate her so much?

"I just want some space, Mom. Some independence." He sighed heavily. "This Parents' Day thing is lame anyway, and this weekend…I'd rather we not do it. Okay?"

She frowned, hurt. "I don't mean to embarrass you, Jason."

"You're not," he said quickly. "It's just that—I get to be different here? I need that. You've said that yourself."

She nodded, looking past him in the direction his friend had gone.

"Of course."

"And I'm going to see you next week anyway," he added.

"It's all right," she lied. "I love you, Jason. I understand."

She hugged him and he let her, his irritation giving way just a little. "I love you too, Mom. I'll see you next week."

She nodded as she watched him go, her pain just another thing she had failed to protect him from.

* * *

There was a diner near the school, The Peter Pan. She pulled into the lot outside and cried for a moment, just letting her emotions run. Why did everything seem to end up in loss? What had she done to deserve this?

She wiped her face dry and looked in the mirror. She'd have to be sure to go home early; she didn't want Lawrence to see her like this. In the meantime, The Peter Pan looked cozy and welcoming.

She went into the diner, sat down in a booth, ordered coffee and took a sip of the bitter black drink.

Her attention was drawn to a flash of ebony hair outside the window. Sarah looked out at the woman crossing the street, her face obscured by her long, beautiful dark hair. Slender, long-legged, purposeful in her stride—even with her face hidden, the woman was almost shockingly glamorous-looking, entirely out of place in the little town. Sarah's blood ran cold as she realized who it was.

*Juliette.*

What was she doing here? Eric wasn't even here—had she followed Sarah? Had she seen her with Lawrence?

The waitress was nowhere to be seen. Sarah rummaged in her purse, found a five-dollar bill, and threw it on the table. A few of the other customers looked up as she ran from the diner, the glass door banging behind her. She looked around just in time to see Juliette slip into a little deli across the road.

Sarah crossed the road after her, ignoring the sparse traffic.

A car swerved around her, its horn blaring; Sarah heard the driver shouting obscenities at her as he went past. *So much for small-town courtesy*, she thought. She ran into the deli, preparing herself for battle.

An older woman walked laboriously through the aisle, pushing a half-full basket on the floor ahead of her with her foot. A man stood at the counter, buying cigarettes from a boy behind it who looked like he was in his teens. Juliette was nowhere to be seen.

Sarah went up to the counter. "Is there a back door to this place?" she asked. The man buying cigarettes turned to look at her.

"Y—yeah," the kid said, staring. "But that's only for employees."

Sarah turned and saw it. Employees Only. She made for the door.

"Ma'am—ma'am!" the kid shouted after her. The older woman stopped to watch her pass.

"What the hell's she—" she heard the man say as she pushed through the door. She passed through a small, messy office, then out another door to the parking lot. Sarah looked around the lot: two empty cars, a broken basket, a dumpster with a few bags of trash beside it.

There was no one there.

* * *

By late afternoon the sun was low on the horizon. Sarah and Lawrence walked around her property, the green hills soothing and the air soft against their faces. It was a large piece of land, and he took her hand as they continued through a wooded area, the trees surrounded by drifts of fallen leaves.

She had kept the sighting of Juliette to herself. It had been a jarring experience, not quite reconcilable with reality; she could have sworn she'd seen the girl, but the others in the deli had confirmed that there was no one there. How had she been so wildly mistaken?

Could her grief from the run-in with Jason really have blinded her so completely? Eric's words came back to her: "unstable," "unreasonable." Had she been wrong about Juliette all along? Surely not; the pieces were all there, too tightly fitting to go together in any other way. But what exactly had she seen, if not her?

She looked at Lawrence, willing herself to concentrate on him instead. Being with him again had dispelled some part of the misery and confusion she felt; he seemed the only light spot in this darkness. The time she'd spent away from him today had been disappointing and disorienting. He was strong, gentle, patient, beautiful—all the things she felt she wasn't. The thought of parting filled her with despair.

"I wish we could stay here longer together," she said.

"Agreed," he replied, holding her closer.

"What happens now?" she asked, afraid of the answer.

He stopped and kissed her. "You're not getting out of this so easy. The park, Monday?"

She laughed. "I'll be there, same old bench."

"Our bench," he corrected her.

They walked on, and soon a thought struck her. "Come this way," she said, pulling him behind her. "I want to show you something."

She led him through the trees to a pond. The water was still, a mirror reflecting the dark sky. A rowboat was tethered by the dock; swans floated serenely by.

"This is amazing," he said, gazing across the water.

"I know. I love this place, especially here." Sarah smiled, remembering. She pointed to the water. "Swans are so majestic. It's one of the reasons I loved this house so much. I've always found them very romantic. You know they find a mate and stick together?"

"They can be cruel, too," he said.

"Cruel? Why?"

"They kill to protect their nests."

Sarah laughed uncertainly. "I never heard that before."

"It's only when they feel threatened," he clarified. "I've heard they attack people pretty often, though it's usually in response to something."

Just then, two of the swans flapped their wings and, with much effort, skidded forward on the surface of the water, lifted and flew off. They watched the birds disappear.

"Beautiful things are often the most dangerous," Lawrence said, pulling her closer. "You have dangerous taste. I'd better be careful."

She punched him playfully on the arm. "Me too," she said.

* * *

Later, after nighttime had engulfed the day, they played with danger together. He'd taken a silk scarf and tied it around her wrists, tethering her to the bedposts. He'd licked her body slowly and deliberately, bringing her to orgasm easily, then had kept her tied up. She succumbed to him in ways she'd never thought she could.

She enjoyed the total loss of control; she relished the trust she felt for him, the courage it required to give over her body and mind so completely. She'd never felt more confident in her nakedness. Even her misgivings were exciting. That their return home might mark the end of what they'd shared—and the affair would bring ruin to her marriage—were part of what she relinquished to him, what she sacrificed for this momentary pleasure.

Leaving her panting, Lawrence sat up to look at her. In the haloed moonlight shining around his muscular body he was almost featureless, a man of shadow.

"I love you," he said quietly.

"I love you, too," she heard herself whisper back. In that moment, her hands bound above her and her body enveloped in darkness, her future as uncertain as it had ever been. She knew it was true.

# PART TWO

# REALITY

*The world, or the state of things, as it actually exists*

# CHAPTER 12

# MONDAY, NOVEMBER 12, 2018

*Sometimes she had hallucinations, she imagined herself buried at the bottom of a tomb, in company with mechanical corpses, who, when the strings were pulled, moved their heads, and agitated their legs and arms.*
THÉRÈSE RAQUIN

"Mrs. Rock, are you all right?"

It was the older detective, Detective Duke, who was asking now. His voice was calm, quieter than his younger partner's. He studied Sarah, his head slightly turned to one side. "Is this woman someone you know?"

She stared dully at the photograph in her hand, her vision coming back into focus.

"No," she finally managed. "I, uh—I don't know her."

"Are you positive?" Detective Schmidt asked. He gestured toward the photo. "Take another look if you need to."

She paused, pretending to study the picture as her mind

whirled. Surely, she could tell them she'd *been* to the park? She'd been there every day this week after returning home, after all—after yoga, while running, before another guarded get-together with Laura. She had done so much to distract herself from Lawrence's absence; she'd come up with every excuse she could to look for him there.

"I mean, I may have seen her," she lied. "She looks like one of the other moms I've seen at the park. But I can't be sure. There are so many people who come through that park." Sarah realized that the mom with the blond child was the woman in the photograph they were showing her. She panicked.

"So you *do* know her," Detective Duke said.

"No—I don't know her. I said I may have seen her, but I don't know. If it's the woman I've seen, I saw her in the playground with her kids," she added quickly.

"When would the last time be? When you may have seen her?" Detective Duke probed.

"I really couldn't say," she said. That was certainly true; even this week, with all its expectation and disappointment, had passed in a blur. If she hadn't rescheduled her appointment with Dr. Robin for today, she probably wouldn't even know it was a Monday. She seized on the idea. "It probably would have been before one of my sessions, maybe a few weeks ago."

"Sessions?" Detective Schmidt repeated.

"I visit a therapist on Tuesdays, sometimes Thursdays."

"Where in the park would you have seen her?"

"The playground. The one on Ninety-sixth Street, off of Fifth."

"Do you go there often?"

"Not too often," she lied again.

"Do you remember seeing this woman there alone?"

"No, with her kids," she said. "Like I said. I mean, I assumed they were her kids. I don't know anything about her." She looked uncertainly at Eric.

"You have children yourselves?" the older detective asked, looking down at his notebook.

"Yes," she said. "Two, a boy and a girl."

"How old?"

"Darcy's twelve and Jason's fourteen—almost fifteen."

"And they were with you in the park? When you may or may not have seen this woman?"

"No," she admitted.

"Where are they now?"

"They're both at boarding school upstate. Cole Manor."

"Were you with someone else at the playground, Mrs. Rock?" Detective Duke asked.

Her mouth went dry. "No. I was reading a book, by myself. *Thérèse Raquin*. You know, Zola, the French writer." Why was she telling them this? "Sometimes I chat with people there, but I usually just sit there to be outside."

"At the playground?" the detective said, raising an eyebrow.

"Yes," she said. "Just outside it. I find it calming, watching the kids play." Eric stared at her, his eyes narrowing, and she felt her face redden. "Why are you asking *me* all this?" she said, trying to stay calm.

The detectives both shook their heads. "We can't really say, Mrs. Rock," the younger one said.

"Why not? Did someone tell you I knew her?"

"It's an ongoing investigation," said Detective Schmidt.

"This woman's been missing for almost a week now,"

Detective Duke said, his voice more relaxed. "Her family's worried. We're just trying to collect as much information as possible." He took the photo back from her. "Her name's Hannah Marie Turner. She has two kids and a husband, Ben Turner. Those names mean anything to you?"

Sarah shook her head numbly.

*B&H. Amor vincit omnia.*

"Do you mind taking a look at one more picture for us?" the detective was asking, still friendly. "Just in case a different one might jog your memory." He handed another photo to her. Her fingers trembled, and she almost dropped it.

It was the woman again, this time on a hike with her kids and husband. Her husband was handsome with stormy blue eyes.

The husband was Lawrence.

Sarah's legs turned weak, and the room became very warm. She looked at the photo again. Same smile, same piercing eyes—same gray jacket he'd had on in the park and at her house. It was him. But how?

"Anything?" Detective Duke asked.

"No," she answered quickly. Had she said it a bit too loudly? "I don't recall seeing them." A thought, cold and horrid, crept into her mind. "When was the last time she was seen?" she asked.

"About a week ago," the younger detective said.

Her heart beat louder.

"Sorry I can't be more helpful."

"No problem," said Detective Duke. For a moment his eyes seemed to sparkle, then they softened again into a smile. "We're going to be on our way, but we'll be in touch," he said. He reached into his breast pocket for a card and passed it across the table to her. "If you remember anything else, or see Hannah again at the park—even if you just think it *might* be her—give me a call. Okay?"

"Of course," Eric said.

"I will," Sarah managed.

"We appreciate you taking the time."

As they left Detective Duke looked back through the doorway at her for an instant, his eyes penetrating.

\* \* \*

She found it easy enough to explain herself to Eric afterward. She only had to tell him that she was lonely and spent time at the park to vary her routine a bit.

Harder to explain was where the police had gotten her name from. Even if someone had seen her at the park, how would they have known to report her? She knew that it could have only come from Lawrence. Ben. Whatever his name was.

*Amor vincit omnia.*

Had she seen Hannah and Lawrence together? Had they ever been at the park at the same time? She couldn't remember; anyway, she felt she couldn't trust the memories she had. Every question Eric asked her felt like hazardous terrain, somewhere her own lack of clarity might trip her up.

Fortunately, she didn't have to explain herself to him for long. Even after a visit from the police, he was soon on his way out, leaving his wife alone again. Today, she could hardly even pretend to care.

Once left alone, she opened her computer, the pressure in her chest almost unbearable. She searched online for *Ben Turner New York, Hannah Turner New York,* mothers' groups, writers,

writing groups, book clubs. *Amor vincit omnia.* She parsed
through thousands of results, hundreds of false starts. Published
Turners, hiking Turners, Turner sisters in Paris. No one came up
who looked even remotely like Lawrence. She tried to remember
if he'd said anything that could help her pinpoint him but could
come up with nothing.

It was as though he'd never been there at all.

She crossed the room in a panic, found her bag, plunged
a hand in. Meeting a soft resistance there, she withdrew the
object from it and clutched it to her chest, feeling her panic
give way to relief.

It was Lawrence's scarf, the gray scarf he'd shown up in in
the elevator. Manuel had found it in the lobby and given it to
her a few days after she'd returned, the very picture of discre-
tion. Never mind that it was thick with Lawrence's masculine
smell; never mind the intensity of Sarah's blush as she'd taken
it, remembering the other scarf he'd tied her hands with during
their last night together. The doorman really was good at his job;
it had been impossible to tell what he was thinking. Thinking
she was going to see Lawrence the following day, she'd kept it
in her bag all week. Its weight seemed to increase along with her
anxiety as the days passed with no sign of him.

Now it turned out it was his wife who was missing. Had he
gone off somewhere with her? No; there would be more than a
single missing-persons report in that case. She remembered the
argument she'd overheard between the two of them, up at the
country house; could he have done something to get rid of his
wife and fled? Sarah couldn't imagine him going on the run or
doing anything even remotely like that.

Her knowledge of him was ridiculously scant—limited to

what he'd told her and what she felt for him. Her euphoria from their trip together had been so strong, she would have accepted anything from him. Without understanding why, she had already lied to the police about him. With a cringe she realized that in the hours she'd spent waiting for him, it had never once occurred to her that she might not be the reason for his absence.

Outside the window a thick fog had rolled in, as if someone had pulled a curtain down over the outside of the building. A few lights shone faintly through it. She saw stirring in the fog, as though a figure was walking past the window, impossibly high.

She pulled the curtains shut and waited in the darkness for time to pass.

# CHAPTER 13

*When they seated themselves in their carriage, they*
*seemed to be greater strangers than before.*
**THÉRÈSE RAQUIN**

Dr. Robin was dressed in a Prussian blue suit with a new pin on her jacket: a gold peacock with blue-and-green feathers. Sarah was more eager than ever to see her. The call to reschedule had been mercifully easier than she'd anticipated, and she was looking forward to telling the therapist all about everything that had transpired the day before. She needed to make sense of everything; if she came clean to Dr. Robin, surely everything else would fall into place.

But Sarah had hardly gotten settled before the therapist spoke.

"Sarah, I should tell you that I know about the police visit," she said.

Sarah sat in stunned silence.

"They came to visit me yesterday," the therapist continued.

"Why would they do that?" Sarah asked, her voice trembling.

"They wanted to ask me about you."

"But how did they know *anything* about me?"

Dr. Robin looked down at her notes.

"I'm afraid I don't know that," she said. "Our conversation was not a long one."

"Christ, I don't even *know* this woman!" Sarah exploded. "She was just some lady I'd see in the park sometimes. I have absolutely nothing to do with her!"

"Had you ever spoken to her?"

"No. I mean, maybe I nodded hello—I don't remember." In her mind she saw flashes of Lawrence and Hannah Turner, arguing. "It wasn't important enough for me to remember!"

The therapist looked concerned. "What about the man you spoke with in the park? Lawrence? Did he know the woman?"

Sarah's stomach knotted, a heavy lump dragging on her heart. She sat up a little straighter. Her hand went for the name-plate on her necklace.

"How the hell should I know?" she said. "I don't know much about him at all, much less who he knows and doesn't know."

"Think, Sarah," Dr. Robin insisted. "You know the answers."

Sarah stared at her. The silence was deafening. "What?" she asked.

The peacock pin glinted as the therapist leaned in closer, expectant. "Sarah, I know this is hard for you," she said gently. To Sarah's amazement, she abruptly got up and sat beside Sarah on the couch. She'd never done it before. "But I want you to tell me honestly. Really think."

"About what?" Sarah said. She could barely hear over the throbbing in her ears.

Dr. Robin placed a hand on her shoulder. "That man in the park," she said quietly. "Sarah, are you sure that he's real?"

The tension ran out of her with a laugh. "Real?" she asked, incredulous.

The therapist's face was deadly serious. "Yes, real."

Sarah laughed again, shaking her head. "Of course he was real. Why would you ask that?"

Dr. Robin stared at her, doubtful. She felt herself gripping the nameplate like a lifeline. *High waves. Have to hold on.* She relaxed her grip, sat up a bit straighter.

"Yes," she said again. "He's real."

"And your relationship?" Dr. Robin asked. "Is *that* real?"

Sarah shook her head. She couldn't believe this conversation was happening. "Do you think I'm making this up?" she asked.

The therapist leaned back a bit. "Sarah, we've been here before," she suggested gently. "Remember?"

The room closed in. Was she dreaming?

"Remember what?" Sarah whispered.

"I've given you every opportunity," the therapist said, a pained expression on her face. "And you'd stopped for a while. But a month ago, he started coming up again."

"He?" Sarah shook her head. "What the hell are you talking about?"

Dr. Robin got up and crossed to her desk. Reaching into a drawer, she pulled out a CD and passed it to Sarah. It was labeled *LAWRENCE* in neat block handwriting. Sarah traced the name with her fingers, unable to speak. She realized that her hands were trembling.

"It's one of our many audio sessions," Dr. Robin was saying. "Whenever I hypnotize you I tape it—but you signed the consent forms, you know that."

She vaguely remembered. "But—this," she said, holding the CD. "Did you tape it when I told you about him?"

The therapist smiled. "I tell you each time you're here to see me, but you don't seem to register it anymore," she said. "Do you recall *any* of it? It does just keep happening, Sarah—you're ruminating."

"Ruminating?"

"It's why you're here. We're trying to make sense of your disorder together."

*Disorder?*

"I don't know what you're talking about," Sarah said. Spontaneously, she rose from her seat. Where was she going?

"Sit down," Dr. Robin said with surprising force. "Sarah, you suffer from a number of delusional disorders. The one at hand is a particularly well-worn one for you: erotomanic disorder, to be precise."

"Eroto-*what?*" Sarah stammered. "I've never heard—"

"Erotomania." Dr. Robin repeated. "And yes, you have. Many times. I explain it to you almost every time we see each other. It's usually women who suffer from it—a woman falls in love with a man with whom she has little or no contact and comes to believe that the feeling is mutual. It is my specialty. It's why you came to me in the first place, so I could help you. There is no right amount of medication to fix this. It's incurable, but with therapy and some medication we can manage it. But you have been one of my most difficult cases."

Sarah sank back into the couch, her mind reeling. "Incurable?" She could not believe what she was hearing. She knew one thing for sure, Lawrence was real. "He was there. He *told* me he loved me."

Dr. Robin walked over to her computer and inserted the CD. "Listen for yourself," she said.

A moment later the doctor's voice came through the speakers.

"*Today's session: May 8, 2016,*" it said. "*Sarah's delusions are intricate, and long-lasting—they've continued for over twelve months now.*"

Sarah gasped and covered her mouth. "That's two years ago," she said.

Dr. Robin nodded, holding up her hand for silence.

"*Her husband fears he may have lost her,*" the therapist's voice continued. "*We're going to talk about them again today. Isn't that right, Sarah?*"

Sarah heard her own voice answer, quiet and faraway. "*Yes.*"

"*Very good. Sarah, I'd like for you to tell me about this new friend you've met.*"

"*He's just someone I see in the park sometimes. He likes to talk with me about books and writing. And he makes me feel different, alive. I feel like I've known him a long time. Do you ever feel that way?*"

Sarah listened, absolutely still with fear.

Dr. Robin's voice spoke again, passing over the question. "*What's his name?*"

Sarah wanted to shut her ears, to block out the answer she knew was coming. "*Lawrence,*" her voice said. "*He's perfect, really. Says all the right things. He makes me feel very special.*"

"*Do you find that odd at all? That this stranger just comes up and talks to you in the park?"*

There was a pause. When Sarah's voice spoke again, it was smaller, hesitant. *"No. Why would I?"*

*"Is he real?"* Dr. Robin's voice asked.

*"Of course he's real."*

"I think we've heard enough," Dr. Robin said. She stopped the recording. "You've been manifesting this relationship for a long time, Sarah."

Sarah stood up again, a black octopus reaching its long arms out of her from within. Impossible. This was impossible. She paced back and forth, the edges of her vision quivering.

"But I just met him," she said. "It was a few weeks ago. He's real. We were—" A cold thought hit her. "This is some kind of trick," she said. "How do I know you haven't altered my voice, made it up somehow?"

The doctor's face barely registered surprise. "Why would I do that, Sarah?"

"I have no idea." Sarah shut her eyes, pressed her fingers to her temples. This had to be a dream.

"It's a psychosis, Sarah. It's not something you can control on your own. It's quite literally your truth, although it has no existence outside you. You normally come in and speak about Lawrence, then he disappears for a while, then you're back to seeing him again. This time, though—this time there's this new person, this woman from the park. You never mentioned her to me before. If we're going to help you, we need to figure this part of it out together."

Dr. Robin sat down beside her again and tried to take Sarah's hand in hers. Her grasp was warm—not at all cool and clinical as Sarah might have expected. Still, Sarah cringed and pulled

129

her hand away.

"Eric—he wants to get rid of me," she cried.

"No one wants to get rid of you. Eric tried to help you. We've all been doing all we can to help you."

Sarah shook her head violently. "Why would I do that? Why would I make all of this up?"

"Trauma is a very powerful thing, Sarah. These delusions can be mood-congruent; they're brought on by trauma and re-triggered by intense feelings like depression. You suffered a terrible trauma when you were young. In your case, that was enough."

Sarah thought back to her childhood, to those lost years. Could her parents' death have been too much for her to process in any other way? "That's impossible," she said weakly.

"It most certainly isn't. It's very rare, but it's far from impossible." The therapist's eyes narrowed. "Why did you stop taking your medication? Your symptoms have been impossible to miss. I can't make you take your medication. But I do believe that with the proper work here, we can help you. If that's going to happen, I need you to listen to me."

"He is real," Sarah whispered, shivering at the memory of his touch. "Lawrence is real."

"I know you *think* he is. And the man himself, whoever he is, certainly is real. But whatever relationship you've created with him—that's fiction, Sarah. Just like the fiction in your books. You've even given your lover the name of a fictional character—Lawrence, Laurent. How can you not see that? You keep reading the same book over and over again, maybe hoping for a different outcome, the ending is always the same. Now I need you to focus on what's *real*. Can you do that?" Dr. Robin leaned in again. "What happened to that woman in the park?" she asked.

"I don't know." Sarah shook her head again and again. "I don't know her—I don't know what happened to her!" The panic was uncontrollable; she felt it take hold of her.

*Run.*

"You have to try and remember, Sarah. You mentioned her to me several times."

"I couldn't have—"

"You *did*. We can play back the tapes if you need assuring. But I don't think you do. Now please." The therapist's tone softened, but the blood pounded harder in Sarah's ears. *Run. Run.* "You're the only one who can stop all of this."

"I'm stopping it right now," Sarah cried out, jolting up from her seat. She made for the door.

"Wait, Sarah!"

Dr. Robin reached out to stop her, but it was too late.

ENTRY, NOVEMBER 13, 2018
Patient: Sarah Rock
Age: 39 (Dob: 12/7/1978)

Sarah's delusion reached a new boiling-over point today. Her psychosis has obviously worsened, counter to my beliefs up to now, and must be addressed in a more drastic way.

The wife of Ben Turner, the basis for Sarah's friend "Lawrence," has gone missing. I am certain Sarah knows what happened to her, but unless she will allow hypnosis in one of our sessions, I don't think we're going to get at the truth easily; her defenses are much too well-established.

In light of the overwhelming nature of the delusional process affecting her total life experience—marked delusions of persecution, grandeur, jealousy, and self-deprecation, as well as complex ideas of reference and agitated behavior—cognitive therapy is no longer going to be adequate in Sarah's case. I believe she poses a danger to herself and others now, and in cooperation with the police, I will move to commit her to a facility that can help her.

Cf. Eliza Thompson: Eliza had been stalking a man who she believed was in love with her. She'd worked for him for five years, then began to confront him unexpectedly and proposition him. Her husband brought her in for treatment after she was fired. Similarly to Sarah, Eliza suffered from PTSD and mood-congruent psychoses. De Clérambault syndrome is associated with an unaffectionate relationship with father. Difficult to treat and chronic.

CHAPTER 14

*Nothing could be more heartrending than*
*this mute and motionless despair.*
THÉRÈSE RAQUIN

Sarah found her way home, into her room, to her desk. She opened her computer, then stared out the window, a woman in a maze. There was only one way out; she knew it.

She had to find him.

*B&H—Amor vincit omnia.* Love conquers all. A thought occurred to her, baffling in its simplicity.

She tried "Turner" and "Latin." She didn't have to scroll down far.

There he was.

He was a Latin teacher in a high school in Manhattan, the Circle School. There was a teacher bio: he'd graduated from Bard

College, grown up in Milwaukee, had a sister and two kids. He was working on his first novel.

She wrote the address of the school down, grabbed her coat, and ran out without locking the door.

* * *

She arrived at the address and got out of the car, walking by the security guard with a friendly "hello," as if she knew him. He nodded, unsuspicious. She certainly looked like a parent.

The elevator took her to the second floor. A young receptionist waited behind a desk, her face open and friendly. Sarah's heart beat faster.

"May I help you?" the woman asked.

Just then, two men appeared at the end of a corridor, talking. One of them was Ben Turner.

Sarah looked at him in shock. Without saying a word, she began walking toward them.

"Excuse me," the receptionist began, getting up.

Sarah didn't stop. "It's fine," she said. "I'm looking for him."

Ben turned toward her, surprise on his face.

"What are you doing here?" he said.

"Lawrence," Sarah pleaded, torn between horror and relief. He was real; at least that was true. She reached out for him.

Ben's face grew heavy and hard. "Olivia, please call security," he said firmly, looking to the receptionist.

"Of course," the receptionist said, going for the phone. The other man backed away.

"Security? What?" Sarah said. Who was this man? Where was the man she knew?

Ben's voice was cold. "You're the woman who was staring at

us in the park," he said, rage overtaking him. "Where the hell is my wife?"

"And why are you here and not out looking for her?"

Sarah felt the room darken, raven wings spreading around the walls. "Lawrence. Why are you doing this?" she begged.

"Lawrence?" the other man asked doubtfully.

"That isn't even my name," Ben shouted.

"Why would you do this?" Sarah whispered. Two security guards appeared in the corridor. She backed away. "You said you loved me—you came with me to my house—"

"What house?" Ben stared at her, wide-eyed. "I don't know the first thing about you, except that you were obsessed with us. Why were you watching us?"

"I wasn't—" she insisted.

The guards grabbed Sarah. "Come on, lady, let's go," one of them said as they pulled her toward the elevator. She looked back at Ben.

"I'm calling the police," he seethed.

"Lawrence!" she shrieked. "I don't know what this is—but I know it was real! I'm not crazy—" She tried to reach into her bag for the scarf, but the guards pulled her arms back.

The guards guided her into the elevator. She looked past them; the other teacher was trying to calm Ben down.

Ben was saying, "I told her to leave us alone, but—" His voice broke with emotion. "Now she's missing, and—"

The elevator doors slid closed.

* * *

She ran from the building, barely hearing the admonitions of the security guards. Her mind spun, retracing what she had done with Lawrence. Had she made him up anew from one day to the next, each time fixating on a different man? Grasping in her bag, her hand sought out the scarf inside. That, at least, was solid; that was not in her head.

She took the train to the neighborhood she had visited with him a few weeks back. As though by intuition she found the bookstore, The Cat and the Owl. Several other patrons were there browsing; turning to look at her when she burst inside. The store felt dark and dirty, losing the charm it once had. Sarah looked around, somehow thinking that she would see a different Lawrence standing there among the shelves.

She recognized the same clerk from before and approached him.

"Excuse me," she said to him. He looked up slowly. "I was wondering if by chance you remembered me. I was here about two weeks ago with a man. We—"

"*Thérèse Raquin,*" he said. "The classic, lust and murder! Did you like it?"

Sarah was relieved. "Thank God," she breathed. "So you do remember me."

"Not a lot of people read Zola," he said, smiling. "I always remember the clients with the best taste."

She nodded hopefully. "Can you remember anything about the man I was with?" she asked.

"Man?" asked the clerk.

"About this tall," she said, holding up her hand for measure. "Dark hair, blue eyes. He bought me the book."

"Sorry, but I didn't see a man." The clerk shook his head apologetically. "I just remember you."

Sarah's heart dropped into a dark hole.

"But—he bought the book. He brought me here—he's one of your regulars."

The clerk shook his head again. "No, you paid for that book. You came in alone. I remember because I watched you—you seemed to know exactly what you were going for."

*No. No. No.*

"I wasn't alone. Please, try to remember," she pleaded, leaning in over the counter. "You have to."

The clerk looked alarmed. He backed away from the counter. "I'm going to have to ask you to leave now, ma'am."

Sarah clutched her bag tightly, looked around in panic as she backed away. The other patrons were eyeing her now, alarm and pity mingled in their faces. In the corner of the store, she spotted a security camera.

"I'm sorry to bother you," she said abruptly and ran from the store.

* * *

Her way home was confused. The train ride seemed a subterranean nightmare, crowded with hostile faces, and she emerged a station early, disoriented and alone.

She found her way to the playground, to her bench. She sat and took a deep breath. She needed to calm herself, to think clearly. She counted backwards from ten to one, closing her eyes and concentrating as she had done with Dr. Robin.

*She saw herself in the park, watching Lawrence. He was talking to a young woman. They were fighting. He grabbed her arm. Sarah gasped, started to walk over to them. She asked if everything was all right; Lawrence turned on her, annoyed.*

*"Mind your own business," he snapped.*

Sarah opened her eyes. Was this the same park, the same bench? Everything seemed different to her: that safe, whole feeling she'd experienced here before was gone. Even the trees seemed menacing now, their branches heavy above her.

She closed her eyes again.

*She saw Eric. She was arguing with him, crying. She was Hannah; Hannah was her. She saw Juliette and Eric together. He was kissing her, Juliette, while Hannah looked on.*

Had she actually seen them together? She stood and walked farther into the park to the reservoir, looking out over the small lake spreading out in front of her. Small waves rippled across the dark blue surface. She thought of blue eyes, deep and agitated, a storm on the horizon. She saw a shadow passing nearer to her. She turned her head slowly.

It was Eric, his face understanding. He had followed her there. At the sight of him, her strength drained and she fell to the ground.

"I am crazy," she sobbed. "I am, Eric." She wept on the ground, her body limp. "I'm so sorry."

She felt his strong hands find hers. "Let's go home, Sarah," he said, helping her to her feet. He put an arm around her to guide her home. "We'll figure it out together. It's all going to be okay, I promise."

She felt relieved to see him there; he was her anchor after all, and she missed that. She nodded and followed him. Together they left the park.

* * *

As they turned onto Park Avenue, they were met with a commotion. Bright lights blinked as they approached their building.

She looked up, no longer capable of being surprised. The lights were from police cars; the police were there for her. She glanced at Eric who stared straight ahead, resolute. Manuel stiffly held the door for them, a look of strained silence on his face.

Inside, several police officers were waiting in the lobby. One of them came forward as they entered.

"Sarah Rock?"

She froze and nodded.

"Please come with us," he said firmly.

Eric nodded to her, strangely calm. "Call Frank when you get to the station," he whispered. "He'll know what to do." He squeezed her hand as another of the officers stepped forward to separate them.

She let them guide her out the front doors, looking back only once at Eric. He looked after her, his face a mask.

"Tell the kids I love them," she called out to him.

The officer's grip on her arms tightened. Sarah's heart sank as she turned, unsure when she would see her home or her husband again.

# CHAPTER 15

*Like certain devotees, who fancy they will deceive the Almighty,*
*and secure pardon by prayer with their lips, and assuming*
*the humble attitude of penitence, Thérèse displayed humility,*
*striking her chest, finding words of repentance, without having*
*anything at the bottom of her heart save fear and cowardice.*
**THÉRÈSE RAQUIN**

The room was not as cold as she might have imagined it would be. The metal chair, however, was ice-cold; she shifted in her seat, trying to find a comfortable position.

Across from her, the two police officers shifted too, hardly any more comfortable than she was. Dazed, she heard their voices as though through a fog. She felt like she hadn't slept in years.

She had texted Frank like Eric had told her to. She'd known Frank Mancini a long time, had practically grown up alongside him. He was big and took up a lot of space. He was lion-like: loud and aggressive, with a full head of curly hair that had turned iron gray over the last few years. He wore a perpetually rumpled dark blue suit that made him look like he lived roughly. Impulsive-seeming in the courtroom and here in the police station as well. He had a good heart and a brotherly soft spot for Sarah. She knew she could count on him.

"She's told you all she knows," he was saying now in his strident, abrasive voice. "She had no connection to that woman."

Ignoring him, the officer tried to press her further. "What was your exact relationship with the victim's husband?" he asked.

Frank looked at her, shaking his head.

"Don't answer that," he said.

Turning to the police, he added calmly, "We'll get bail on this. She's not a flight risk, nowhere near it. She's got kids."

"Mrs. Rock, this could be extremely easy for you," said the other officer. "All we need to know is—"

Frank stood up, his frame imposing in the small room. "That's enough," he said sternly. "Are you charging her? This is all circumstantial, and you know it."

"Tell us about the tree," the policeman said, ignoring him.

Sarah blinked. "What tree?"

"The one on your country property."

"What about it?"

"You said you were going to plant a new one or take care of the old one. Why was that?"

"You don't need to answer any of this," Frank warned her.

"It's all right, Frank." She thought of the beautiful tree, broken in two. "The tree that was there was damaged from the storm, six months ago. It was just something I needed to take care of."

"It's also irrelevant," Frank insisted, "like everything else you keep asking her. Listen, unless you're charging her, she's not going to be answering any more questions for you." He reached for Sarah's arm. "Come on, Sarah, I think we're done here."

"Just a minute," the cop said, not moving from his seat.

The officer slammed photographs of Hannah's body lying on leaves with a bloody wound on the side of her skull. Sarah could see a shadow of a tree in the picture.

"Mrs. Rock, you do understand that's where we found her body?"

Sarah stiffened.

"That's right." The officer nodded, as though he were explaining something to an idiot. "Her body. Hannah's body."

"Oh my God," she whispered.

"This is what I'm trying to tell you, Mrs. Rock," the officer said. "She was found under your tree, the one on your property. Didn't you say you were there last week? Don't you think you'd better tell us about that?"

Frank held out his hand to calm Sarah. "These are empty threats," he said. "There isn't any—"

He stabbed his finger at Sarah. "There's a body in *her* backyard! We have witnesses saying she stalked this woman. So please don't tell me we don't have a fucking leg to stand on, counselor, because we do!"

Sarah was in shock. What was Hannah's body doing in her backyard? None of it made sense, she thought.

The officers placed photographs in front of her of Hanna's dead body lying on leaves.

"Are you charging her or not?" Frank said impatiently. "My client is under great duress. We need to consult her doctor as well. We only agreed to this interview to help you; everything you've said is circumstantial. If you were charging her, you'd have read her her rights by now."

"This is only going to get harder for you, Mrs. Rock," the other officer promised. "And as far as your therapist goes—Dr.—Helena Robin, right?" He flipped to a page in his notebook. "We've already spoken to her. She told us you may have thought that the victim's husband had a relationship with you. She thinks maybe you were obsessed him."

"I wasn't," Sarah said.

"Then what were you doing?"

"We had a relationship. A real one."

"You and Ben?"

"Yes."

"An affair?"

"That's enough!" Frank shouted. "Here's what you have: a dead woman buried in my client's backyard. So what? Anyone could have put her there, and you know it. Not a single witness can corroborate what you're suggesting, except circumstantially. And we're going on the word of the husband, with whom even *my client* admits she had an affair. Shouldn't you be questioning *him?*"

"Don't worry about him," one of the officers said. "We're talking to him, too. But so far, his story's looking a lot more credible than hers."

Exasperated, Frank helped her to her feet. "We'll be going now," he said.

"Door's unlocked," the officer said diffidently.

Frank led her out. "It's going to be okay, Sarah," he said softly. "They've got nothing. Next time, you just keep on telling them, 'Get me my lawyer' until they stop talking."

They walked out together and stood outside the station. Frank held her for a moment, comforting her.

"I know you're confused," he said. "But please, do not talk to anyone about this, especially this Ben Turner guy. Do you understand me?"

Sarah nodded. "Why haven't they arrested me yet?" she asked.

"They will as soon as they can, trust me," he said. "I don't want to scare you, but for now, you need to stay home. Any reason they can come up with, they'll do it." He ran a hand through his gray mane. "I'll take you home, and you should try to get some rest. We can talk again in the morning."

She squeezed his hand. "Thanks. Can I speak to the kids, at least?"

"Not now." He held onto her hand and looked her straight in the eye. "It would be better if you didn't put them through this right now," he said, quietly but clearly. "I think they should stay at school this weekend, if you can keep them there; it'll be better for everyone. I'll take care of everything. Put your phone on silent, and get some rest. Talk to that doctor of yours, if you can."

"One other thing, Frank." She leaned in close, reaching into her pocket. She drew out the bookmark she'd taken from the bookstore. "I was with Lawrence—Ben—in this store. The week before we went up to the country house. When I went back, they didn't remember him, and I was sure he was lying—but I saw a security camera there. That should prove that we were there together. Please."

Frank looked down at the address on the bookmark. He sighed.

"I promise I'll look into it," he said. He hooked his arm into hers. "Now let's get out of here."

As they walked past the precinct, a silhouette in an open window caught Sarah's eye. Something about the man seemed familiar. She squinted to look.

It was Ben Turner, apparently waiting alone in an office inside the police precinct. He looked out the window at her, his face impassive.

Her eyes never left his. He glared back at her, his once-soft eyes now steely and unyielding.

"Come on," Frank said, almost picking her up to move her away from the window.

She burst into tears as her attorney pulled her away. How on earth would anyone believe her over the calm, collected-looking man in that office? For a nightmarish second, she doubted herself, too.

As she passed the open window, the steely look in those blue eyes broke—and Sarah saw the tiniest smirk cross her former lover's face.

# CHAPTER 16

*Thérèse, residing in damp obscurity, in gloomy, crushing silence,
saw life expand before her in all its nakedness, each night bringing
the same cold couch, and each morn the same empty day.*
**THÉRÈSE RAQUIN**

That night, Sarah dreamt of the eyes.

She had seen them at Coney Island, on a day when she had taken the children out for a special afternoon on the rides. They had driven out to the boardwalk, excited and jumpy. Eight-year-old Jason had been asking to go for months; all his friends had gone already, he'd said. He didn't remember visiting as a baby; she barely remembered it herself. And of course, what he wanted, Darcy wanted. Coney Island was the glittering treasure that they were after that summer.

It had been a sunny day on the coast, hot and sticky despite the ocean breeze. As soon as they had arrived, she saw crowds of people gathering in herds along the boardwalk—they ate mindlessly, their jaws laboring as they lumbered forward. The sun shone on pink foreheads, tanned arms glistening with sweat, and salt-wet hair. It had been impossible to walk in a straight line. In the distance the sand shimmered, slick like a mirage.

She stopped to buy tickets for one of the rides. When she came out of the shade, Jason and Darcy were gone. She looked frantically along the snaking lines, calling their names loudly. The noise around her had grown louder: music and announcements, screeches and hisses from the rollercoaster rides, babies crying, teenagers shouting. The noises had blended together in a sickening swirl, and she felt the world spinning around her.

A face leaned in, far too close, and in that moment, she had seen the eyes.

The man they belonged to was dressed in a colorful costume, a clown or a performer. Had there been a parade? His face glistened with sweat; wet stains ran along the seams of his costume. She recoiled from him, but he had only smiled wider, his teeth yellow and crooked. She felt paralyzed, but, incredibly, he'd been friendly, helpful: he'd taken her arm and brought her around a corner to a booth with uniformed people. They'd paged Jason and Darcy and brought the three of them together again. The children had only been gone a short time, and they were unafraid.

She was terrified. Helpful as he had been, there was something in the man's eyes that had struck her with fear. She had seen something horrible that she recognized: an irreconcilable craziness, a chaos that threw her own fear back at her, mocking her loss even as she was frozen with sorrow and despair. It was something she would see again at the worst moments in her life;

the moments when her fear left her with nothing to do but stand, stock-still, and stare helplessly at her reflection in the mirror. It was the madness she recognized in herself.

\* \* \*

When she woke, it was past midnight. She looked around and saw that she was in her own bed, still wearing the same clothes from the day before.

Her head pounding, she went to the bathroom and opened her medicine cabinet. All of her medications stared back at her. Had there always been so many? She found the aspirin and popped two in her mouth, letting their bitter taste sit on her tongue a moment before washing them down with water.

She could hear Eric in the kitchen, clanging around. She imagined him pouring a beer, settling in for some evening sports with a bowl of chips and guacamole. The thought comforted her, if only slightly: something was as usual.

She opened her computer and searched online for *delusional disorder*. Pages of articles appeared. Eyes glued to the computer, she clicked on one of the results and read to herself.

> Delusional disorder is a mental illness characterized by false beliefs about external reality that persist despite evidence to the contrary. Symptomatic of psychosis, it is usually treated with medication and extensive cognitive therapy.

As she read, images of herself popped into her mind. She saw herself approaching Lawrence in the park, the two of them embracing. She shook her head pushing the images away, searching through other articles.

> Primary erotomania or de Clérambault's syndrome is a
> delusion most commonly found among women, generally
> manifesting as the false belief that another individual, usually
> a man, is in love with them.

She heard Eric moving around, now in the living room, and
paused. The noise ceased, and she continued reading, her eyes
darting around the screen.

> ...most famous case involved a fifty-three-year-old French
> dressmaker who was convinced that King George V was
> deeply in love with her. She pursued him relentlessly, and
> when he ignored her, she would say he was in denial and
> accuse him of being involved in...

The noises started again. Had Eric said anything to her when
she'd come home from the precinct? She couldn't remember.
She clicked back to the previous article.

> Delusions are imaginary situations, most of which are based
> on events that could occur in real life. Typical examples
> include the persistent sense of being followed, being loved,
> or being...

She heard a noise behind her and spun to find Eric there.
"What did you tell them?" he asked.

"Nothing," she said, shutting her computer. "There was
nothing for me to tell."

His eyes were serious. "You know that isn't true," he said.
"*What?*"

"It isn't true, Sarah. You know it, and I know it."

"What are you talking about?" She looked at him. "I'd never

hurt anyone, you know that."

He waited for her to go on.

"It was him," she said. "I know it. He used me, Eric."

"Used you how? How could he have done that?"

"Too easily." She felt her eyes welling up and knew it was time. "I'm sorry you have to hear this, but yes, I had an affair," she said. "It didn't mean anything—I needed something to make me feel like I existed." The words and tears poured uncontrollably. "I haven't been happy, Eric. You know that. You go on these trips—and I *know* something happened between you and her, it's obvious, so—"

Eric shook his head sadly. "Think, Sarah," he said. "I know you can remember."

"What do you mean?" she cried, confused. "I told you, I didn't touch that woman! How could you think I am capable of anything like that?"

"You *are* capable of it, Sarah."

"How can you say that to me?"

"Because it's true!"

"What the hell are you talking about, Eric?"

Her husband threw his hands up, exasperated. "You tried to *kill* Juliette!" he shouted.

There was a long silence. Sarah sat down hard on the bed.

"You don't remember?" he went on. "Of course you don't. It was before I left for the Atlanta trip. You were convinced that I was cheating on you. But I never did that. It wasn't me, Sarah. Your father—" His voice trailed off.

"My *father?*" Sarah echoed, her voice breaking. Images shot through her mind: an open door; Eric and Juliette sitting at a table; herself, screaming at them.

"He wasn't there for you. For either of you. But I have been."

She squeezed her eyes shut and saw her father. A strong, handsome man with dark hair and dark eyes; a stormy sky. She saw him leaving, walking out; in another room, her mother cried hysterically.

"You stalked her for months, Sarah," Eric went on. "Don't you remember any of that?"

"No, I would never—"

"You attacked her." His voice was quiet but firm. "You were choking her. I had to stop you. Don't you remember doing that? Don't you remember the struggle we had afterwards, the help we tried to get you? Do you think Dr. Robin was the only therapist we went to?"

Sarah shook her head. "I remember, there were others. But I didn't trust them."

"She was the only one willing to try something other than having you committed!" he cried. "She was the only one who didn't give up on you. Besides me."

"You want me out of here," she said. "You want me gone, you want me—"

He came closer to her, his face pleading. "I want you to be the woman I married again. It's all I've ever wanted, Sarah."

Sarah turned and saw her disheveled appearance in the mirror. Her face seemed nightmarishly different, the face of a stranger. None of this made any sense.

"Then why are you gone all the time?" she screamed. "If that's true and you want to salvage this, why the hell are you never here?"

She broke down, sobbing. She thought she heard Eric come closer and anticipated his hand on her back; in her mind she saw him comforting her.

When she looked up, she was alone, with only her reflection looking on: a distorted version of herself.

\* \* \*

Dr. Robin agreed to meet with her again. It had to be brief, she said, as she had another engagement to go to after—but Sarah didn't care. She had never been so relieved to see the therapist. They talked for a while before the doctor retrieved a folder from the filing cabinet next to her desk. She handed it to Sarah, a serious look on her face.

"What's this?" Sarah asked.

"It's all there. I thought we'd made progress. Perhaps we had. Are you ready to talk about your parents now," Dr. Robin coaxed.

Sarah opened the file reluctantly. It was filled with photocopied documents and photographs. On top was a folded newspaper clipping dated March, 1986.

"You've remembered bits and pieces over the months," the therapist said.

Sarah looked closely at the photograph of the little blonde girl whose smile so strikingly resembled Darcy's.

"This is me," she said, almost in disbelief. "This girl is me."

The therapist nodded. "Your father seems to have been a very handsome and charismatic man," she said. "Your mother was very young. They were married after you were born."

"He wasn't happy," Sarah said, remembering. "It was all because of me."

Dr. Robin shook her head. "He was depressed and scared and selfish. It wasn't your fault he left."

Sarah shook her head, pulling out the clipping to look more closely at the photo. "She cried all the time. I can still hear her."

"She coped for as long as she could. She worked very hard to make excuses for him. But that wasn't enough." Dr. Robin nodded again, encouraging her. "Do you remember what happened then, Sarah?"

"The accident—"

"No, Sarah. What *really* happened?"

Sarah blinked back tears. What was she supposed to remember? "They died in an accident, both of them. That's all I remember."

"Look at the picture again," Dr. Robin said. "Imagine yourself as that little girl, Sarah—try to imagine the last thing you remember seeing."

"The last—?"

"It happened in your house, upstairs. You've told me about it many times before, Sarah; I know you can remember again."

She looked at the photo, at the girl she could hardly remember being. She would have been younger than Darcy then—just eight years old.

She remembered the gunshot. And then the blood, her scream, and her mother's empty stare.

"She—" Sarah faltered. The words stuck in her mouth: her own disbelief—the scene not making sense to her; the silence afterward; the empty house.

She saw it all, saw what she had forced herself to forget. "She killed herself," she whispered, while trembling. "Right in front of me. My grandparents—they took me," she continued.

"Yes."

"But how—I never remembered—" Sarah began.

*Teresa Sorkin and Tullan Holmqvist*

"The brain works in miraculous ways," said Dr. Robin. "It shields us from danger. But that shield peels back sometimes, and we get glimpses of the past. After a trauma like that, almost anything is possible."

Sarah unfolded the clipping to read the headline on the other side.

### WOMAN, ANNABELLE JULE, FOUND DEAD IN BROOKLYN APARTMENT

Late Sunday evening, neighbors called the police after finding a young girl wandering the hallways of their Brooklyn building, searching for her mother. Annabelle Daltry Jule, 28, had taken her life, leaving an eight-your-old daughter, Sarah.

Witnesses and neighbors described Annabelle as happy and well-mannered. Annabelle had raised her daughter on her own since her husband, Richard Jule, left the family. The girl has been placed with Social Services, pending the location of Richard Jule or other family members.

Services will take place at the Tanner Funeral Home on Tuesday at 3:00 p.m.

Other photos were in the folder: her mother; their apartment building; herself being carried away by a police officer, her face emotionless.

"I remember an entirely different childhood," Sarah said, shaking her head in disbelief.

"As a child, you created your own reality," the therapist went on. "The trauma was too much for you to deal with."

"But my grandparents—"

"Your grandparents were suffering too and indulged it. It wasn't until you married and had your own children that some of that repressed past started creeping in, asserting itself. And then what happened with Eric opened it all up again."

Sarah nodded. Juliette, of course. The affair had dredged everything up.

"I created an alternative reality for myself?" she asked. "Since I was *eight?*"

"You did—and no one got you the help you needed," Dr. Robin went on. "Your grandparents did the best they could, but they were ill-equipped to confront your delusions while dealing with their own loss."

Sarah looked at the picture of her mother. She'd been so young and beautiful—how could he have left her; how could he have hurt her so badly?

"He was a monster," she whispered.

"He was a man," Dr. Robin said. "He made mistakes. It was your mother who truly abandoned you by killing herself."

"I hated her," Sarah admitted. "I hated them both. He was—"

Something became very clear in her mind, she was unsure how she'd ever forgotten it.

"His name was Lawrence," she said. "My father. I remember how much we loved him. He looked like a movie star. She called him her Cary Grant. They used to dance. It made me so happy to see them like that."

Dr. Robin nodded. "You idolized this idea of him," she said. "It's what you would later use as the basis for your erotomania. It's not uncommon—it's called delusional fixation. Something about Ben Turner reminded you of your father—the way he looked, or how he interacted with his wife. It stirred up some memory within you, and you latched onto it, the hidden logic being that by keeping him in your life, you will ultimately keep your father and save your mother. But Ben was only one of many. There have been others."

She retrieved another file from the cabinet and placed it in Sarah's hands. Inside were several closely typed, formal-looking pages: harassment complaints. Each had a different name at the top.

"These were all because of me?" Sarah asked, incredulous.

Dr. Robin nodded.

Sarah leafed through them. All the complaints were similar; the same words turned up again and again.

"Stalking." "Following." "Harassment."

Sarah let out a breath. "Have you told me about this before?" she asked.

"I'm afraid so," the therapist said.

"And I never remember?"

"You always do for a little while." Dr. Robin smiled faintly. "Then you regress again. But this time was different."

"This time the man's wife ended up dead," Sarah blurted out. She remembered a glimpse of Ben—Lawrence—in the park, yelling at Hannah. Had it actually happened? Or was it her he'd been yelling at?

"Yes." The therapist nodded gravely.

"I would know if I did something like that, wouldn't I?" Sarah pleaded. "*You* would know."

"I can't say. You've been fighting me so much, Sarah."

"There were things I know happened," Sarah insisted. "It's

impossible that they didn't. We went up to the house together, ate there together. We made love there. He knew about the tree—I told him."

"It's not impossible that you experienced all of that in your head."

"That vividly? How can that be?"

"This kind of delusion is very strong," Dr. Robin said. "Mood-congruent psychoses can be overpowering, especially when they're linked to equally strong feelings of loss or unhappiness. Your feelings in relation to Eric and the kids have been that trigger for you. It's a classic triad of depression."

Sarah felt a chill run through her body. *Triad of depression.* Where had she heard that phrase before?

"I'm sorry," she said slowly. "A classic what?"

"Triad of depression," the doctor said. "Beck's cognitive triad, or negative triad, as it's commonly called: negative thoughts about oneself, about one's future, and about the world. Triad of depression is my term for it. In your case, the effect it has on the psyche is to encourage the kinds of fabrication we've been talking about."

Sarah barely heard her. She was remembering where she'd heard the phrase before.

Lawrence. He'd said it on their trip together.

"I am sorry, Sarah," the therapist continued. "I feel that I've failed you. I wish I could have done more." She looked down at her hands. "Naturally, I have to cooperate with the police, but whatever I can do to help you—"

Just then, they heard the muffled sound of a phone ringing. Dr. Robin looked toward her handbag.

"Let me silence that," she said awkwardly.

"No, it's okay," said Sarah, alert and on guard. "I know we need to wrap up anyway. Take the call—I can wait."

"Are you sure? I imagine it's nothing."

Sarah gave her most apologetic, nothing-else-to-do smile. "I'm not going anywhere."

"All right."

The therapist took her handbag and walked out of the room.

*Triad of depression. My term.*

It was Lawrence who'd said it before. Sarah was sure of it. But what did that mean? Sarah had to find out if there was some connection.

She'd just settled herself on the couch again when Dr. Robin returned.

"My apologies," the therapist said. "I'm going to have to get going."

"It's all right," Sarah assured her. "It was so good of you to meet with me today anyway. Just one thing." She eyed the doctor carefully. "About those CDs—the ones you recorded of me. Do you think I could listen to them? Now that we're discussing all this?"

Dr. Robin shook her head, her face contrite. "I've had to give them to the police," she said. "I'm sure your lawyer will be able to get copies for you, but it's out of my hands for the time being. You've made major strides, Sarah. You're taking responsibility for your life. One way or another, I know you'll be better off than you were before," Dr. Robin said.

Sarah barely registered their last goodbyes as she noticed Dr. Robin lock the cabinet that contained all the answers she was looking for. Dr. Robin placed the keys on a tray on her desk.

When Sarah left, she crossed the street to a coffee shop and took a window seat, so she could observe when Dr. Robin left her building. She ordered a tea while she waited to make her next move.

# CHAPTER 17

*Thérése experienced no hesitation. She went straight where
her passion urged her to go. This woman whom circumstances
had bowed down, and who had at length drawn herself up
erect, now revealed all her being and explained her life.*
THÉRÈSE RAQUIN

Ten minutes later, Dr. Robin exited her building and walked
down the block away from her office. She seemed to be in a
hurry. *All the better*, Sarah thought.

Once she was gone, Sarah walked back to the doctor's office
and the receptionist was not paying attention as usual.

"I forgot my phone in the office, can I go get it?" Sarah said.

The receptionist waved her in without looking up.

Once inside, she went directly to the desk and picked up
the keys to the filing cabinet that were in the tray. She opened
the cabinet and flipped through file after file, the multitude of
names seemingly organized not alphabetically, but by type of

disorder. She looked through files and found a section labeled "EROTOMANIA."

She found a file marked S. ROCK right next to another labeled E. THOMPSON. She peeked into the other folder: an Eliza Thompson. It might be worth looking up one of Dr. Robin's other patients. Sarah didn't know exactly what she was looking for, but she was hoping that the other patient would have some answers. She opened the file and saw a photo of a young woman with dark hair and intense eyes staring back at her.

She heard a noise from next door and froze. Was someone coming? Sarah took both files. She waited a few minutes in total silence, hearing footsteps pass in the hall. She breathed easy again. She'd need to hurry; getting caught would be a disaster for her.

She opened the next drawer. Three rows of CDs. Dr. Robin had lied about giving them to the police, Sarah realized. She quickly found the ones marked with her name and took those. She stuffed the files and CDs into her bag and gave one last look around the room. She doubted she would see the inside of this place again.

Doing her best to seem casual and collected with her full bag hanging from her shoulder, she locked up and left.

\* \* \*

The Brooklyn townhouse looked like a happy home, at least from the outside. Clean steps led up to the front door, flanked by pumpkins; the windows were lofty and—rare for New York—free of bars. It wasn't the sort of place Sarah would have associated with a delusional mind. But then again, her own home wasn't either.

She double-checked the address against the file, then replaced it in her bag, walked up the steps, and rang the doorbell. A very small young girl answered, her face wary. Sarah knew from the file that this was Eliza's daughter. The file didn't provide as much information as Sarah would have hoped, except for detailing the symptoms of erotomania, which mirrored her own. Sarah had to try and find Eliza to find answers.

"Hi," said Sarah, as cheerfully as she could. "I'm here to see your mom," she guessed. "Eliza."

Without a word the girl ran into the house, closing the door behind her.

Sarah waited for a few moments, then knocked again. Nothing. She reached for the door, realized what she was doing, and pulled back. Was she really prepared to walk uninvited into a stranger's home, a home with a child inside?

Just as she was turning to leave, the door opened. A tall man stood there, a stern expression on his face. He needed a haircut and a shave. Sarah had seen mentions in the file of Eliza's husband, Damien Thompson; this must be him.

"Who are you?" he asked bluntly. He had a sad face, handsome behind the heavy lines: there was something there that reminded Sarah of Eric.

"Sorry to drop in on you like this," Sarah said. "Are you Damien?"

"Yes," the man said dubiously. "And you are—?"

"My name's Cynthia," she lied. "I'm a friend of Eliza's, from—"

"No, you're not," he snapped, interrupting her.

"I'm sorry?"

"If you were, you would know that she's away getting help,"

he continued.

She felt her skin prickle.

"Goodbye." He began to shut the door in her face.

"Please—I need your help," she said quickly. "I'm another patient of Dr. Robin's."

The door opened again, and the man's expression softened. "Helena Robin?" he asked.

The small girl peeked out from behind him.

Sarah took a deep breath. "I'm sorry to lie, I've been seeking treatment with Dr. Robin recently, and I'm a little concerned about her. I had some questions about—"

"You're right to be concerned." Damien gave a sardonic half-laugh. "She treated Eliza for years."

"Yes," Sarah said. "But she's away now?"

"That's right."

"So Dr. Robin wasn't able to help her?"

Damien half-laughed again. "Quite the opposite," he said. "Seeing Helena Robin made her worse, much worse. We had to commit her."

"Oh my God," Sarah said. "I'm sorry."

"She's doing better now than she was before, that much I know."

"How exactly was she worse before, if you don't mind me asking?"

"It came and went," he said. "When it was bad, it was really scary. She said she'd met a man but didn't know his name or anything about him because he liked to keep it a mystery. We wanted her to go away for a bit, but Dr. Robin dragged it out. If I were you, I'd keep away from her."

Sarah felt a chill go through her at the mention of a man.

"What do you mean, she dragged it out?" she asked.

"She said Eliza needed more time. She said she'd be able to help her with hypnosis sessions. We trusted her at first, but she only made it worse. Eliza became more paranoid and detached than usual—spent more and more time in her own delusional world. Eventually, I decided to get her the help she *really* needed. That's when we had her booked in at Margo. She seems to be improving there, though it's slow."

"It sounds like you did the right thing. She's lucky to have you," Sarah said, making a mental note of the name.

"It takes a toll. I married her for better or for worse, but this illness—" He noticed the little girl behind him. "You seem friendly, but I don't think we can be of much help."

"It's all right," she said. "I can't imagine it's easy for you, talking to me like this."

"It's our life." He smiled at the little girl behind him. "Try to keep it from becoming yours. And keep away from that so-called doctor. She's incompetent, at best."

Sarah nodded, thinking of Darcy. "I appreciate it," she said.

Damien shut the door, his little daughter peeking curiously out until the last moment. Sarah was shocked that her doctor was possibly making things worse. She knew that if she wanted more answers, she would have to go see Eliza.

\* \* \*

The ride to the Margo Mental Hospital was a long one. When she reached the hospital, she hesitated outside.

Making up her mind, she strode in. If this was where Eliza Thompson had ended up, it was at least worth finding out why, and what shape she was in.

The security guard behind the desk was young, and Sarah smiled confidently as she walked up to him.

"Hi," she said breezily. "One of my patients is a resident here, and I need to speak with her. Her husband called me earlier this afternoon."

The guard looked at a logbook in front of him. "And you would be Doctor—?" he asked.

"Robin," said Sarah. "Helena Robin." She leaned over the counter, following the guard's finger down the list. "I'm sorry, I know it's after-hours."

The guard studied the list carefully. His finger had stopped at a numbered line—302. "Dr. Robin, you said? I don't see you on my list of approved doctors."

"I was her old doctor—I'm also a family friend," she said. "This is a confidential matter, but it won't take long—I'm sure I'll be in and out in ten minutes."

The security guard shook his head. "I'm sorry. I just can't let you in without it being approved, and it's too late to get approval today," he said. "If you come back tomorrow, we can straighten it out with the supervising doctor on duty."

Sarah bottled her disappointment. Time to try a different tack.

"If you insist," she sighed. "I told her husband—but I understand. Thanks anyway, I'll come back tomorrow." She hesitated, giving him a charming smile. "Can you tell me if there's any place to get coffee around here? This comes at the end of my day, and I have a long ride back to the city."

Warming up he said, "I get that—I have the night shift, too. It's killer the next day."

"Awful! The body just never gets used to it."

He pointed towards the back of the building. "There's a cafeteria in the back. They're still open but only for another fifteen minutes." He smiled. "If you hurry up, I'll let you in to grab a coffee."

"That'd be great," she said, leaning forward flirtatiously.

"It's the least I can do, turning you away like this," he said.

"Thanks so much." She started down the hallway. "And I will see you tomorrow," she said over her shoulder.

"Hope so," the guard laughed back.

When she looked back and saw that he had turned away from her, she slipped into a stairwell and bolted up the stairs to the third floor, taking out the patient files as she went up.

The third floor was quiet. A nurse at the nurse's station barely acknowledged Sarah as she walked quickly past, eyes buried in Eliza's file. She quickly found room 302 and peeked in. Through the window in the door, she saw a young woman, pretty and frail, wearing white pajamas and watching television.

Sarah knocked lightly as she pushed the door open and walked in.

"Eliza?" she asked. "Eliza Thompson?"

The woman turned to look at her. "Yes," she said slowly.

"I'm Sarah." She didn't know where to sit, so she just stood still and let the door close behind her. "I was wondering if I could talk to you. I hope I'm not disturbing you?"

Eliza shrugged. "I'm just watching the *Housewives*," she said. "Seems to be the only show that makes me happy these days. Those bitches are crazier than I am."

Sarah laughed in spite of herself. Eliza smiled, too.

"Are you really here?" Eliza asked, looking at the files in Sarah's hand.

"I'm sorry?"

"Well, I *am* delusional," the small woman said, matter-of-factly. "Or didn't they tell you?"

Sarah smiled. "I'm really here," she said.

"All right." Eliza held her hands up. "What do you want to talk about?"

"I was hoping you could tell me about your therapist, Dr. Robin," Sarah said.

It was like a switch had been flipped. Eliza's face became dark.

"She ruined my life," she said simply.

Sarah flinched. "Can you tell me how?"

"She fucked with my head," Eliza said. "Damien and I were going to get me hospitalized early on, but she convinced us that she could help. She kept me in hypnotherapy sessions for months, convincing me that all this shit was in my head when it was really happening to me."

Sarah's blood ran cold. "Why was she doing that?" she asked.

"I was one of her guinea pigs. She experimented on me. She even used one of her other patients to lure me into a relationship so she could test me. Problem was, she didn't count on me telling my husband the truth. And then I realized she was fucking her patient on top of all that," Eliza said. "She should be the one in here, but of course, she is trying to tell everybody that I'm lying and it's part of my delusion, but it isn't."

"What was the man's name?" Sarah questioned.

"Who are you again?" Eliza demanded.

Sarah blinked. "I'm sorry, I'm a new doctor."

"No you're lying."

Immediately it felt as though all the air in the room had

gone out.

"It's never been easy for me to know what's real—I doubt myself all the time. Sometimes I don't even know if *I'm* here. By the time I was onto what she was doing, I'd already done too much crazy shit for them to believe me," Eliza said. "That's when I ended up here. That's the hardest part for me. That bitch won."

Sarah took her hand. "She won't keep winning," she said. "I promise you that."

Eliza looked at her uncertainly. "Who did you say you were?" she asked.

Suddenly, looking into Eliza's eyes, she saw something she recognized. Eliza's face wavered, her eyes drifting in mirage-like tears. As Sarah watched, they became the eyes of her mother, apologetic and hopeless.

"I'm sorry," Eliza said. "I didn't mean to leave you."

Sarah felt a draft pass through the room. The hairs on her arms stood on end.

"What did you say?" she asked, shaken.

The vision faded, and it was Eliza she was speaking to.

Eliza leaned back, again on her guard. "I said be careful," she repeated. She drew her hands up protectively, seeming to shrink into her chair. "I think you'd better leave."

Sarah's phone vibrated in her pocket. She glanced at a text message that came through. The message was from Frank: "Where are you? I just got a call from Dr. Robin looking for you. Call me."

Panicked, Sarah thanked Eliza, then turned and dashed out of the room.

* * *

She walked as quickly down the hall as she could without running, so as not to draw attention to herself. The nurse at the station again ignored her, absorbed in her phone. She really had to get out of there before someone noticed her.

At the end of the hallway, she opened a door into a stairwell. The air around her seemed to be spinning. She saw strange colors and heard noises, both faraway and too close. She had to hold onto the banister to keep herself from falling.

She heard a familiar voice behind her.

*"Sarah!"*

She flew down the steps, two at a time, panting heavily. She heard a familiar voice behind her, "Sarah!" Risking a glance upward, she saw the security guard and Dr. Robin racing down the steps after her. What was she doing here?

She continued down, the footsteps closing in. She ran to the end of the stairwell and pushed through the basement door.

She had gone too far: she found herself in a large boiler room, hot and dank. From the center of the room she heard hissing and sputtering sounds, a dangerous snake waiting to strike. From behind her, she heard the footsteps descending the last few stairs.

She slid under an enormous metal casing and held as still as she could, her breathing heavy and her heart beating like a drum. The casing was hot against her coat; she felt she would faint if she had to remain here for long.

The door opened and shut several times. She heard shuffling back and forth in the room, panting breaths. Below the casing she saw the guard's shoes run past then Dr. Robin's boots. She held her breath and waited.

When the noises had receded deeper into the basement, she crawled out and slowly opened the door back out into the stairwell. No one was there. Sarah's mind was reeling with all the information she had heard, she was spinning, she had to retain her grip on reality long enough to tell Eric all she had learned. She closed her eyes and started counting backward to herself.

She felt hands grab her bag and pull her back into a tight grip. She screamed and fought against the heavy arms holding her. A hand covered her mouth and she bit down hard. The man released her and she spun around to face him. It was Ben Turner, his eyes wide with fury.

"Get away from me!" she shouted, charging forward to knee him in the groin.

He fell back with a grunt against the steps. She went back down to the boiler room and picked up a length of pipe leaning against one wall. Ben followed but stopped when he saw the pipe.

"You need help," he said, his voice mechanical. "I'm here, Sarah. I've only ever wanted to help you."

She waved the pipe at him, horrified. His face was a blur— now Lawrence, now Eric. She blinked to clear her vision.

"Don't come any closer," she hissed.

"Don't you remember how I made you feel?" his inhuman voice grating and raspy. "Don't you want that again?"

His feet seemed to disappear into the shadow at the edges of her vision—and she understood. He wasn't real. He wasn't there.

She closed her eyes, willing him away. She thought of her children. They were real; she was real.

When she opened her eyes, Lawrence was gone. But she knew Dr. Robin was real and was still out there looking for her.

171

She had to get out and home to Eric.

She quickly walked out to the stairwell, then up and out to the cool air of the evening.

CHAPTER 18

*But inwardly, she lived a burning, passionate existence. When alone on the grass beside the water, she would lie down flat on her stomach like an animal, her black eyes wide open, her body writhing, ready to spring.*
THÉRÈSE RAQUIN

She found another cab home and fell asleep on the ride, exhausted and confused. On the ride, she dreamt of the winter Darcy turned six.

Eric had arranged a special ski vacation in Colorado, a "real winterland adventure," he'd called it. None of them had wanted to go. He had planned the trip as a surprise for the family.

She had been furious with Eric. Darcy was a sensitive child with a delicate constitution; she was always coming down with colds, inexplicable leg pain, and stomachaches that kept her in bed for days. At the time, Darcy had just recovered from a series of coughing fits that had lasted for weeks. Her pediatrician had recommended vacations to warm, humid places.

Eric had grown up skiing and missed it terribly. He loved the mountain air and the vigorous exercise; he wanted the kids to love skiing and to be as good at it, too. "The tired legs, the achy muscles—you'll sleep like logs," he had promised them.

They landed in Colorado and drove up the windy road to Telluride. It was beautiful; the sharp-edged peaks surrounded them, high and clearly visible in the freezing sunshine. It had felt like they were entering a secret world, an ice-fairy paradise.

Within an hour, Sarah had come down with a splitting headache. Eric told her it was just the altitude. Her anger had only exacerbated the pain—but thinking of Darcy, she had swallowed her fury, refusing to burden the others with it. She'd felt dark smoke circling around her, tying her down; she'd gotten increasingly heavy and sad until all she could do was lie down on the hotel bed, curled up with her eyes turned toward the wall.

She skipped dinner that night, and her headache worsened. When Jason came to check on her, she hadn't even had the energy to turn around and answer him. She stayed in bed the following day and the day after that.

The kids had gone excitedly to ski classes each morning, and in the end Darcy skied down the biggest slope, earning a medal from the ski school. She wanted to hug her daughter, swing her around in the air with pride. But her heaviness had only gotten worse, it kept her in bed for the entire week.

It made matters worse that she seemed to be the only one suffering.

* * *

Darkness had long since fallen by the time Sarah opened her front door.

The house, too, was dark. Eric was waiting for her in the foyer.

"Sarah," he cried, reaching out to her.

She collapsed into his arms, bursting into tears. She smelled his familiar scent, felt his arms around her. He would protect her; he always had. How had she been so foolish as to doubt him?

"It was her," she sobbed. "It was Dr. Robin."

"What was?" Eric asked, still holding onto her tightly. "What has she done?"

"She used me," she said. "I talked to another patient of hers."

"Sarah, just—just calm down," he said.

She pulled back from him.

"Are you hearing me? I found her. Her name is Eliza. She can tell you everything." She pulled at her husband's arm. "Eric, please—"

A voice came from the next room: "Enough, Sarah."

Sarah turned abruptly. Dr. Robin was walking toward her, eyes shining.

An image flashed through Sarah's mind, of the man at Coney Island, the man with the madness in his eyes. She backed away from Eric, feeling the blood draining from her face. How could he have betrayed her?

"Stay away from us," she shouted at Dr. Robin. "You lied to me—it was you from the beginning!" She reached for her husband.

She gasped.

Eric was gone.

Only she and the doctor remained.

*"Eric!"* she screamed.

Dr. Robin stepped toward her, her voice calm.

"It was you, Sarah," she said. "It was always you."

"Eric—" Sarah sobbed, staring frantically around the room.

"Ben is my patient," Dr. Robin continued. "You saw him in the waiting room and fixated on him as you did all the others. You believed you were in a relationship and followed him to the park."

Sarah shut her eyes. She saw Lawrence, walking along the pathways of Central Park, oblivious to her following him.

"No," she said, shaking the image from her mind. "No, you're lying—"

"You know it's true, Sarah," the doctor said coldly. "You've done it before. Juliette—Hannah—it's all part of your disorder, these jealous and obsessive thoughts."

Sarah ran into the living room. "Eric—" she cried, looking for him in vain. Dr. Robin followed her.

"He's not here," she yelled. "You need to realize that he's not here, Sarah!"

"What are you talking about?" Sarah shrieked, spinning around. "What have you done with him?"

Dr. Robin spoke slowly, as though she was reasoning with a child. "You know, Sarah," she said. "Dig deep. I know you can."

The darkness moved behind the therapist, and Sarah saw there was a man there. He stepped forward.

"We can help you," Dr. Robin was saying. "But you have to come with us."

Sarah backed away, her eyes fixed on the therapist. "And Eliza?" she said.

"What about her? She told me what happened. You did the same thing to her!"

"There is only one person you can trust, and that person is me. I've been trying to help you this whole time," Dr. Robin said.

Sarah collapsed to the floor. Her head felt as though it would split apart. She put her hands to her temples.

"I have to be better," she said. "Jason and Darcy. They need me."

The man stepped closer, gripped Sarah's wrist.

Sarah looked up at him.

It was Eric. He held her face gently in his hands.

"I love you, Sarah," he said. "You have to let this go. You have to heal. Please. I need you to be okay."

Sarah closed her eyes. The warmth of his love flowed over her and she felt the tears streaming down her face. She saw him in her mind, smiling; she remembered him motionless on the ground.

No. He was here with her.

She felt him take her hand, pulling her to her feet. Something was wrong. She opened her eyes.

Dr. Robin was standing in front of her. Someone else stood behind her, pinning her hands.

*Eric?*

"Come with us," the doctor said and gently guided her toward the door.

Sarah struggled to look behind her. The man was taller than Eric, heavier. Where was her husband? What had she done?

"Eric!" she shrieked.

Then, in the shadows she saw him looking at her, his eyes pitying; the absent husband, the absent father. The man behind her shoved her forward, and she saw the shadow flicker, the image of her husband fading.

She remembered—yet this time the truth was stronger, and instead of him she saw herself, hovering over his body, crying desperately for him to come back. The late nights, the absent mornings, the strange comments from her children, the pitying glances of strangers and friends—it had been right in front of her, all along.

Her husband was gone.

Eric was dead.

# CHAPTER 19

*Hatred was forced to come. They had loved like brutes, with*
*hot passion, entirely sanguineous. Then, amidst the enervation*
*of their crime, their love had turned to fright, and their*
*kisses had produced a sort of physical terror. At present,*
*amid the suffering which marriage, which life in common*
*imposed on them, they revolted and flew into anger.*
THÉRÈSE RAQUIN

She sat in the backseat of a car. Through her swollen eyes, raw from tears, she saw darkness outside, lights flashing past quickly.

She had let the doctor lead her, her thoughts chaotic and confused. Where were they taking her? Did it matter? Perhaps it would be better simply to drift off, to invite better dreams to replace her consciousness; perhaps, if she slept deeply enough, she would never wake again.

Her husband had been gone for six months. It all came to back to her in waves. Sitting at the table with the kids, Eric hadn't been there. She realized Manuel hadn't given Eric an umbrella when it was raining because he hadn't been there.

And had everyone else noticed that she was talking to herself at the party because Eric hadn't been beside her? It was all too unimaginable to accept, but, then again, Sarah couldn't grasp what was real or not anymore.

Maybe the only person she could trust was Dr. Robin.

There was a new sound in the car: a voice speaking to her through the car speakers. Or was it the radio? Sarah looked around; Dr. Robin was in the front passenger seat, not looking back at her.

*"I can't go back to that day,"* the voice said—a stranger's voice, metallic and heavy.

"*You have to, Sarah,*" another voice answered through the speakers. It was Dr. Robin's voice: persistent, forcefully calm. Yet the doctor hadn't moved.

"*How can I?*" the first voice pleaded; and in an instant, Sarah knew that it was her own voice she was hearing.

*"I just want to forget,"* the voice was saying, quieter now. *"But I can't."*

\* \* \*

The car had stopped. Outside it was pitch black now. The back door opened, and Sarah was led from the car. An icy wind blew through the trees, chilling her.

The man moved away into the dark as Dr. Robin pulled Sarah's jacket around her and escorted her down a gravel path. Sarah saw the remains of violets lining the path, soft as velvet still—the herb of the trinity, symbol of true love—and knew where they had brought her. This path was hers; she'd planted those violets. *The country house.* She also noticed yellow tape surrounding their family tree.

"It is still a police scene, and they will be back in the morning. We don't have a lot of time for you to remember everything. I think it's important that you remember," she heard the therapist say, her voice a tired mother's as she unlocked and pushed open the front door. They entered, her feet dragging beneath her like a sleepwalker's.

"It happened here," the doctor was saying. "Do you remember, Sarah?"

"What did?" Sarah asked. She remembered Lawrence kissing her, Eric kissing her, all those days and years ago. For an instant she saw her husband, standing next to the doctor. She shut her eyes, regretting so much.

"Shhh," the therapist said. "Focus. Remember."

The memories flashed through her mind, the past filling her completely.

* * *

*She is by herself in the kitchen preparing dinner. Friends will be joining them later, and the country house is quiet, full of promise.*

*The door opens, startling her. It's Eric, coming back from the city. She's happy to see him, but he is withdrawn.*

*"Where are the kids?" she asks. It is difficult to chop and talk at the same time. She is making penne al ragù, a sauce he loves.*

*"Sarah," says Eric. Even in that brief word, his voice strikes her with its seriousness. Tired, she thinks: work has been very stressful for him lately, and he has so many things to worry about. "We have to talk."*

*"About?" she answers offhandedly. She is thinking about preparations for tonight: the guests, the wine. Where are the kids?*

*"I think you need to go away for a while," Eric says quietly.*

181

*She almost drops the knife. "What?" she whispers.*

*"This obsession. It's been getting worse."*

*Her mind whirling, she realizes. "Eric, where are the kids?"*

*"They're not coming to the house tonight," he says firmly. "I brought them to my sister's." He gathers himself for what's next. "And they're going to go away to school for a bit."*

*"Away?" She panics, throws the knife onto the counter. She spins to face him. "You can't do that without my permission!"*

*His eyes follow the knife as it clatters against the granite counter. Alarm gives way to anger. "They need a normal life, Sarah! This drama—they don't need to be part of it." His voice softens and he steps forward to put a hand on her shoulder. "Your therapy hasn't been helping. We both know that. Juliette isn't going to press charges, but—"*

*Her heart is a burning pit at her center. "I knew it," she mutters. "I knew you were leaving me for her."*

*"I'm not leaving you, Sarah. But this has to change. I love you, but we can't keep doing this."*

*She slumps to the floor, sobbing. Eric picks her up gently.*

*"Sarah, I am not him. I'm not your father, and I never will be. But you aren't your mother either. You have to stop blaming yourself for what happened between them. You have to stop enacting it in our lives." He caresses her cheek. "Please."*

*A thunder crack makes both of them jump. Outside the wind picks up, a storm coming. She looks at him as if seeing him for the first time.*

*"Tell me the truth, Eric," her voice hard. "I know you want to be with her. But I need you to admit it."*

*Eric throws his hands up. "You've stopped taking your medications, you've stopped sleeping. Until you get help, this can't work."*

*"What the hell am I supposed to do?" she screams.*

*"I've looked into some options," he says. "But it can't be at home. You have to go somewhere they can help you." He heads upstairs. "Come on, Sarah. I mean it. We need to pack a bag for you."*

*Her mind races. Go away? Away where? He can't do this to her. Their house is already a prison, its walls closing in.*

Run.

*She opens the door and runs out into the darkness.*

*"Sarah!" she hears him yell after her.*

*She runs aimlessly downhill in the darkness, her feet finding the path to the pond. Lightning explodes, lighting up the sky. She turns to see her husband emerging from the front door, his eyes searching for her.*

*He trips and falls to the ground beneath the tree they planted when they bought the house. Their tree—a symbol of their family's future.*

*Already drenched, she looks up at the tree. Its branches spread out wide, leafless. Beneath, Eric struggles to his feet.*

*Lightning strikes again. The thunder crack is immediate, deafening. For an instant, the tree seems to flash light.*

*Eric's whole body tenses, falls to the ground.*

*"No!" she cries out, already running toward him.*

*She is too late. He lies motionless on the ground. His eyes seem to look up at her, but she knows they are sightless. Above her the lights in the house have gone dark. She looks around for some sign that she is dreaming.*

*She cradles his head and cries.*

*He is gone.*

\* \* \*

"Gone," Sarah said out loud, shocking herself with the words.

She was sitting on the floor now. She looked up at Dr. Robin again. "Eric is dead."

The doctor nodded. "It's been many months, Sarah," she said. "I did my best to ease you into the reality of his death, I let you talk about him as if he were still here, but this is what's real. No matter how much you want him to be here and pretend he is, he's gone."

Sarah protested. "I feel him. I see him. I hear his voice. He is here with me."

"He's dead. You haven't been able to let him go."

"You don't understand, I can't," Sarah's voice broke and tears rolled down her cheeks. "It's a piece of me."

Behind her a shadow moved in the doorway. The man emerged into the light, solid and real.

It was Ben Turner. He stared at her, his face emotionless.

"You were here," Sarah said to him. "I know you were."

He nodded.

"I was," he said. "I was trying to help you."

She shook her head. "How?"

"You had just lost your husband. She suggested that we try something different, and I was willing." He gestured toward Dr. Robin.

"It was such a terrible accident," the doctor said.

Sarah felt weak. Her head swam, and she had to concentrate not to collapse on the floor.

"Why are you here now?" she asked Ben.

"Ben has been my patient for a long time," the therapist said, stepping over to the doorway where he stood. "Just like you, he lost his parents very young and has suffered with bouts of depression."

"She helped me, Sarah," Ben said. "I need her. You do, too."

"I gave him a greater purpose; in helping you, he felt needed. His wife didn't understand him in the way I did," the therapist explained.

Sarah stared in disbelief as Dr. Robin stroked Ben's cheek as though he were an obedient puppy. The image was sickeningly absurd. Sarah felt her grip on reality slipping and held on tight to what she knew.

*Jason. Darcy. The house.*

"You two have actually met before," Dr. Robin continued. "You talked to him in the office a few times when your appointments crossed. He made you laugh, made you seem alive. And we had been trying for so long without results." She smiled, an awkward expression on her rigid face. "I thought, what harm could there be in indulging your little fantasy instead of fighting it? It was a rare opportunity, a new possibility to cure you."

A thick cloud seemed to gather around her words. Sarah felt herself floating.

"There were other opportunities as well," Dr. Robin said. She nodded as Ben picked Sarah up off the floor, depositing her heavily in a chair.

"It's all right," Dr. Robin answered. She pushed a sheet of paper across the table toward her.

"You can relax—you don't have to do anything else," the therapist was saying. "I typed this for you. With your attention to detail, I think it's plausible you would type it."

Sarah squinted at it, trying to understand. The words on the page danced and blurred, defying interpretation.

"It will do your children good for you to come clean about this," Dr. Robin said. She moved to the sink, filled a teakettle. Had she been here before? "They'll know their mother did the right thing. No more running, Sarah. No more fantasies."

As Sarah looked down at the words on the page, a few phrases began to come together.

*I cannot bear to...*

*My obsessions have gotten the best of...*

*Her death at my hands was...*

It was a suicide note and confession.

"This house is so lovely. Isn't it, Ben?" the therapist said. She opened a cabinet and withdrew a teacup. "It's such a shame your past kept you from enjoying all that you had in your present, Sarah. I really did try." The teakettle began to trill, and she took it off the heat. "Hypnosis, regression therapy, cognitive therapy. The meds weren't even that effective when you were taking them properly! You were really an incurable case."

Shaken, Sarah looked again at Ben. "But you—" she began.

"Ben's pattern is not dissimilar to yours in some ways," Dr. Robin interjected.

"But—your wife," Sarah said.

"An unfortunate variable," the therapist said. "Her reaction when she found out about us was less than favorable. She came to my office. She had figured out what we're doing and really, just imagine, your case study would have been legendary had I cured you. So I couldn't allow her to ruin everything."

It began to connect for Sarah. "I was just another guinea pig like Eliza," she managed.

"We did think we could help you. It wasn't supposed to end like this," Ben said quickly. He turned to the doctor, his expression stern.

Sarah's head spun. Could any of this really be happening? She was incredulous. "All this was just part of some *experiment*."

"More than that," Ben insisted.

"But why—"

"Sarah, we all have deeper motivations, desires that no one else knows about or understands: fame, passion, lust, revenge, ambition. You were my ambition, my social experiment. And all great discoveries have their martyrs; history does its best to forget that." Dr. Robin's tone was icy. "There is a long and storied history of psychological experimentation on orphans, for instance. You two are hardly the first. It was an experiment, just like my predecessors, the courageous doctors before me who had to sometimes attempt new methods to get results. Even Dr. Freud conducted his own therapeutic experiments that led him to fame. Sometimes there are casualties for the greater good. I am close to solving this so-called incurable disorder," Dr. Robin ranted.

Sarah shook her head. "But your wife—Hannah—she was innocent," she said. For an instant, Ben's face contorted.

"There's no rule stating that our lives must be fair, or meaningful, or safe. And in the service of discovery—who knows what we might accomplish? When a cure is discovered, do we moan over those who had to be sacrificed along the way?" She shook her head. "The mind is a messy business; what you think of as a simple affair, or an unhappy marriage, can mean much more to the researcher. Barriers to that pursuit—" She stroked Ben's cheek again, soothing his confusion. "It's all right, darling," she whispered. "I'm still with you. We're here together."

Dr. Robin turned to Sarah. "When Hannah came to my office that day after you and Ben had returned from the weekend away, she said she was going to expose me. She had discovered some of my emails to Ben. She wouldn't listen to reason and then became enraged, and she pushed me. When I pushed back to defend myself, she fell and hit her head. I saw the life go out of her, and I just had to clean it all up. That night, Ben and I brought her here."

"So you brought her here and buried her under our tree?" Sarah asked.

"The truth is, Sarah, you were a failure." Dr. Robin drew a small envelope from her pocket and poured the contents into the teacup. She filled the cup with boiling water. "Like other patients before you, you proved intractable, overly rigid. It was time to start over anyway."

She brought the cup to Sarah and set it down by the confession on the table.

"This pain—this confusion and misery," she said. "We can end this together, Sarah. We can make you whole again—reunite you with those you've loved and lost. You've done so much wrong in your life, but we can help you make it right." Her voice was relaxed, an expression of utter peace. "No more agony. No more deception. No more delusion."

Through her tears, Sarah looked at the cup.

"Drink that, and we'll put an end to the mistakes," Dr. Robin said soothingly. "Everything you've done—it'll be all right."

"You've hurt so many people," Dr. Robin continued. "You've made so many mistakes. It's time for that to end."

Sarah picked up the cup, its scalding heat a strange comfort to her. It was so brutal, so meaningless.

She thought of Eric's body, contorted on the ground.

She had never asked for a mind so fractious; she had never

asked to be the cause of so much pain. And it would be easy
to end it: to put herself to sleep and put it all to sleep with her.

She thought of her children.

"They will be safer this way," Dr. Robin intoned, as though
hearing her thoughts. "They will be happier this way." Her hand
caressed Sarah's back, motheringly.

Sarah raised the cup to her lips, smelling the bitterness.

*Sarah.*

She saw her husband standing behind the doctor. He was
as handsome as ever, his phantom smile a reproach to her. He
was all in her head now, a specter waiting to be freed with her.

*No, Sarah.*

She paused.

"I am sorry," she whispered.

"There is no need for that anymore," Dr. Robin said. "Drink,
and put it behind you."

Behind the doctor the shadow of Eric shook its head.

*I love you,* she heard him say. *Do not do this.*

She broke into tears. "But our children—"

*Our children don't deserve what you were dealt. They deserve
you.*

"Your children will be happier without you," the doctor
repeated. She tipped the cup gently toward Sarah's lips. "Now
drink—"

*No!*

Sarah pushed back, shoving the cup away. Dr. Robin put
up her hands just in time to deflect the boiling liquid from her
face, screaming as it hit her.

"Ben!" the doctor screamed.

Ben lunged at Sarah, gripping her arm tightly. Sarah twisted, struggling, and together they fell onto the couch. Desperately, she reached a hand out and grabbed a photo frame. She brought it down across his face as hard as she could.

The glass smashed and Ben cried out and fell backward, blood flowing through his fingers as he clutched at his face. Sarah struggled free and ran up the stairs and into her bedroom, locking the door. She heard the doctor's footsteps race up the stairs after her.

"Open this door!" the doctor shrieked. The door thudded heavily twice.

Sarah raced to the window and tugged at it. It wouldn't open. Outside her door she heard Ben's heavier steps tramping up the stairs. Dr. Robin's voice came through the door, tense between panting breaths.

"Sarah," she said. "This has to stop. There's nowhere left to go."

By the dresser, Sarah found one of Eric's old golf clubs. She remembered the strength of his hands as he taught her to swing, showed her how to transfer all her force to her hands.

"Open the door, Sarah," Ben shouted. His voice was hoarse, monstrous.

Sarah swung the heavy window open and felt a rush of cold air.

The bedroom door rang with heavy blows. Sarah thrust her body through the window pane, scraping her leg on the ledge. Ignoring the pain, she stepped out onto the roof and glanced below. It was a twenty-foot drop to the garden. The ground looked hard.

As she stood out there, Ben broke through the door and ran toward her. She edged backward on the roof, almost losing her balance.

"Stay back," she screamed.

Ben dove for the window, reaching his arm through the glass. She stood up and swung at him as hard as she could, a solid left-hand swing. The club connected with his forearm and Ben screamed in pain, falling backward into the bedroom. Inside, Sarah heard Dr. Robin curse as Ben fell against her.

Flinging the golf club away, Sarah knelt to lower herself from the roof. Her feet found a trellis. Bracing herself, she pushed back and dropped the remaining fifteen feet to the ground. Her legs buckled under her with the impact and she fell to the ground, the force knocking the wind out of her.

She struggled to her feet. A pain shot through her left foot and she almost dropped again. Blood dripped from the cut on her leg. She felt herself growing lightheaded.

The car. She had to get to the keys somehow.

She limped toward the garden shed. If she could only hide inside, she might be able to—

She felt arms around her, pulling her up. Ben was holding her while blood trickled down his face from the cut on his forehead. She turned to see Dr. Robin standing by the front door.

"Bring her here," the doctor said. She gestured, "If you're not going to drink it on your own, Sarah, we'll force you."

As Ben led Sarah forward, she looked around wildly. A glint from beneath one of the bushes near her caught her eye: the handle of the golf club.

"Wait," she pleaded. "Don't do this—you don't have to help her. Your wife is dead. She's just using you. She's done it before, and it hasn't helped anyone. Do you really want her to kill me?"

Ben, stunned, hesitated, while Sarah lunged for the golf club.

She got a hold of the handle as Ben grabbed her arms.

Dr. Robin strode toward her, shaking. "Just drink the tea."

Ben looked at Dr. Robin, easing his grip on Sarah.

"Are you really trying to help?" he asked.

Dr. Robin looked at him. "You know I am helping you," Dr. Robin said forcefully.

Sarah realized her arms were free and charged the doctor. Dr. Robin fell to the ground and her knee snapped with a dull crack. The doctor screamed, and Sarah let the momentum carry her into the doctor and they went down together.

Struggling for the golf club, Sarah grasped the doctor and pulled back, kicking the club out of her grasp. From the pond came the sound of agitated squawking: the swans, seemingly terrified by the screams.

As they struggled, Sarah heard Ben's voice, impossibly calm. *Driven by passion and madness. Just as Zola said.*

In her shock, she looked over at Ben standing there motionless. The voice had been in her head.

Or were his lips moving?

Seizing the opportunity, Dr. Robin grabbed her by the throat and rolled on top of her; her face red with frenzy. She banged Sarah's head against the ground and Sarah saw stars. The doctor's weight pressed down, and she felt her consciousness giving way as the grip around her throat tightened.

Just as she shut her eyes, a gunshot exploded—and the world went silent.

The doctor's fingers loosened, and her body slumped across Sarah's chest.

Sarah screamed; the sound muffled under the ringing in her ears.

"Police!"

The shout had come from the driveway. Sarah writhed under the doctor's limp body, trying to free herself from its horrible weight. Ben stood above her, he put his hands up, letting a Swiss Army knife fall from his fingers. He had stabbed Dr. Robin to save Sarah.

"I trusted her; I thought she was helping me and helping you, I really did," Ben said to Sarah.

Sarah felt sorry for him. He had been just as lost as she had been.

He backed away, his breath ragged. The police approached cautiously, their shouts barely intelligible. Sarah turned to see Dr. Robin lying unconscious next to her. The face that had once calmed Sarah, now a terrifying mask.

In the flashing blue and-red lights of the police cruiser, Sarah caught a glimpse of another figure running toward them: a woman, someone she knew.

The noise and lights overwhelmed her, and she collapsed. In the closing darkness, she saw her husband smiling at her. The cold air blew harder on her face, and the weight on her chest lifted; she was running to meet him.

*Eric. I'm coming.*

* * *

She opened her eyes.

She had to blink a few times to focus her vision. The walls were white, bare, and cold; the air was metallic and smelled like cleanser. Where was she? White, bare—*let it not be Dr. Robin's office,* she pleaded silently, feeling her stomach cramp.

She tried to sit up and a pain dug into her shoulder. She

slumped back in the bed.

She was in bed? What bed?

She closed her eyes. Perhaps she was dreaming. Then she felt a sharp ache in her side and clenched her teeth. No, this was real.

She felt someone touch her arm gently.

"Sarah, just rest." The voice was kind. "It's all over."

She opened her eyes and looked to one side. Laura was there.

Sarah looked around again. The bed had a metal frame; there were wires and monitors nearby. Hospital.

She lay back down, relieved. But—where was Ben? The image of Dr. Robin's lifeless body shot into her mind and she winced.

Laura spoke again. "I saw him, Sarah," she said. "With you that day by the reservoir. I pretended not to, but I saw that you were happy, and I thought you would tell me when you were ready." Tears streamed down her cheeks. "It was so heartbreaking after Eric died. No one knew what to say or do. I'm sorry."

Sarah tried to smile at her, still confused. "Dr.—" she began. "Is she dead?"

"No, but it's over," Laura continued. "They are with the police. I told them everything I knew. They realized Ben had lied about knowing you. I didn't say anything about him earlier, but then I read about the missing woman and saw his picture—I'm so sorry, Sarah. I should have been a better friend. I tried calling you last night and so did Frank. But we couldn't find you. I had a hunch we should come here with the police."

"Ben—Lawrence—" Sarah's voice faltered.

"The police are dealing with it—he won't hurt you anymore," Laura said quietly. "Frank told the police about the surveillance video from that bookstore. You were right, Sarah."

Sarah's eyes welled up. She was vindicated—but at what cost?

"Just rest now, Sarah. Everything's going to be all right."

There was a stirring in the room. Behind Laura she saw Eric. He was smiling at her, pride mingled with sadness in his eyes. She smiled back, seeing Laura's face light up in response. Eric reached for her hand, and she reached for his. When Laura took it, it was his fingers she felt.

Sarah closed her eyes.

# FIFTEEN MONTHS LATER

Winter had descended. The icy snow dusted the park, and the tree outside her window was covered in white. In just a few months, the magnolia tree would be in bloom, its delicate yet strong flowers already budding, white-and-pink, silk-smooth petals sprouting from branches that now seemed dead. She, too, knew it was time to begin again.

It was all she could do.

Crisp air, bright sunshine, a light dusting of snow alongside the road upstate: it was the perfect winter day for a drive to the country. But for Sarah, it wasn't so simple.

She felt right about the sale of the house, but it wasn't going to be easy. She would miss the trees, the pond, the swans with their mysterious, placid lives. She thought of the things that she would collect from the house that day: baby shoes, locks of hair, little prizes and medals, photos and artwork. Mementos of their lives there, keepsakes for her children to have someday. Jason and Darcy would have their own opportunity to collect the things they loved that had fostered their early lives; for now, she would take the things she knew she wanted to hold onto herself. Above all, she would give away Eric's clothes and shoes; those reminders she had kept for too long.

The drive was difficult for other reasons, too. Her body remembered the road, the time she'd been here last. A few times she started breathing heavily, her arms and legs losing strength as she drove. She felt the familiar urge to get out and run in the opposite direction, to disappear. But times were different now, and in those moments she focused on her breathing, reminding herself that she and her demons were on better terms these days.

"Breathe in, breathe out," she repeated to herself. The world's first mantra as Dr. Benz liked to say.

It had taken her a long time to find a new therapist after all she had gone through. It was hard for her to trust anybody. She had finally found Dr. Benz after trying several other doctors. She had felt the most secure when she stepped into his office, it had a calming aura. If he'd set out to make his office an environment completely the opposite of Dr. Robin's, he couldn't have done better. It felt lived in, warm and personal, like a favorite sweater. The furniture was done in tasteful patterns and antique leather; pictures and books lined the walls. Dr. Benz was equally personable, and though they didn't talk much about his life, he was never reticent to discuss it: late fifties, two kids and a golden retriever. Having learned these details, Sarah rarely asked him for more; knowing he was open to sharing was enough.

Dr. Robin and her past had always been a mystery. Sarah learned from the newspapers that Helena Robin had been an orphan as well and then gone from foster home to foster home and was adopted by a psychiatrist who Sarah felt certain had experimented on Helena as a child. Orphans were the best subjects, she would say, because they were the most vulnerable. Sarah was saddened by all of it, but technically she wasn't an orphan herself. Her father, although he had abandoned her, was still alive. And after all that had happened, he reached out to her after reading the story in the paper. He explained to Sarah that he had tried seeing her during all of those years, but her grandparents wouldn't allow it, so he stopped trying. Sarah was taking it slow with him, but she did forgive him and was open to the possibility of having him in her life again.

Dr. Benz agreed that it could help her deal with her past. He also seemed enthusiastic about her idea to sell the country house. Her motivations were the right ones, he said, and he felt it would help to bring her a sense of closure. He had put her visions of Eric into context, too, and even kept the word *delusions* out of his explanations. The condition, which he referred to by the much more neutral-sounding name of Post-Bereavement Hallucinatory Experiences, was not at all unusual among people who had lost a loved one. It was generally understood that seeing and hearing such spectral entities helped people cope with losses they couldn't otherwise handle. In Sarah's case, the sense of loss, and the hallucinatory experiences that accompanied it, were essentially the same thing, but much more markedly pronounced. It was possible she would experience some form of PBHE for the rest of her life, he admitted—but with work such occurrences would never again control her or confuse her.

\* \* \*

On her way up, without any purpose, Sarah stopped at the hardware store, McNally's. Despite her sadness at selling the country house and the horrible things that had led her to this point, it was soothing for her to visit this place again.

She entered the store and wandered through as she always had. Inside, the store was warm and organized; new things could be created here. An inspiration struck her: she would plant new flowers on the grounds before the place was sold. Not just reminders, but renewals.

Among the potted plants she saw a star-shaped flower with long, dark-purple petals accentuated by many yellow stamens. The clerk smiled approvingly as she placed it on the counter.

"Nice choice," he observed. "Clematis is such a beautiful flower. Keep it inside until the snow has melted. It's a climbing vine—it likes to grow upwards, looking for the sun. Monarch butterflies love the leaves, too."

"Monarchs," said Sarah quietly, remembering the butterflies that had visited them every autumn on their way to warmer fields for the winter. "I love butterflies."

"Beauty and transformation," the clerk smiled. "Don't eat the plant yourself—it can kill you."

Sarah laughed, thinking of the other things that could have done that recently. "I won't. I promise."

"So many beautiful things are poisonous, aren't they? You have dangerous taste." The clerk gave her a wink.

"I've heard that before," she smiled back at him.

She'd paid for the flowers and was on her way out the door when the clerk called to her.

"I almost forgot," he said. "We just got some new Swiss Army knives, if you want to have a look?"

She stopped in her tracks.

"Swiss Army knives?" she asked.

He nodded.

"No," she replied quickly. "Thanks, though."

She headed back out to the car. Opening up the back, she placed the potted flower gently in one of the empty boxes she'd put in the backseat. She bent down to slide the box over and noticed a book on the floor beneath the passenger seat. It was *Thérèse Raquin*.

She smiled, not sure what to think about Thérèse. Was she villain or victim? It was impossible for Sarah to answer simply after everything that had happened; with minds like hers and Thérèse's, perhaps those terms didn't quite apply.

In any case, it was time for a new book.

NOTES, DR. AARON BENZ
Patient: Sarah Rock

Sarah was rather serene today. She has been pro-active with her treatment and exercise and looks much happier than when we began. Her memories of the night of the incident are still fuzzy, but that's understandable enough. Her nightmares have lessened, though she seems to be having fewer dreams altogether these days.

I am encouraged by her positivity; she seems to be adjusting well to the new state of things. She has considered putting her family's country home on the market, which seems to me to be a step in the right direction. And her father has come back into her life, possibly healing some of the past pain.

She is still seeing things. I see progress with the hallucinations, especially in telling me about them, but there is still work to be done.

She has planned a trip to Europe with her children—to Florence. She looks forward to sharing aspects of her life with them that she hasn't before: her time in Florence seems to be particularly symbolic of that for her.

\* \* \*

Back in the city, Sarah left her building to go for a jog in the cold winter air. Having missed running while she was in recovery, she'd decided to train for the marathon, and it had become a ritual for her. Dr. Benz had encouraged the new passion. Besides, it allowed her to imbue the park with new associations completely her own. Together with her weekly meditation evenings at the yoga center, she was turning over a new leaf. Coming to the park with a purpose was different; even Jason and Darcy had noticed the change in her. Frank had, in his own chaotic way, become a bigger part of Sarah's life. Some Friday nights, he showed up for dinner with the kids; it was a surprise and it gave her some comfort.

She had discovered the city in a new light. The avenue bustled with people, and she didn't feel as alone as she once had. She explored new areas of the city, even venturing out to the waterfront in Brooklyn. Not far from her building, she saw a young woman on the corner. A jolt went through her as they recognized each other. The woman walked up to her, eager but visibly nervous.

"Juliette," Sarah said softly. "I'm surprised to see you."

"I've been trying to—" Juliette broke off, her dark, beautiful eyes apologetic. She smiled. "You look better," she said.

"I am. Thank you." Sarah took a deep breath. "Juliette, I'm sorry—about everything."

The words seemed to release a floodgate in the other woman. "It was hard at first," Juliette said, her eyes going to the ground. "I felt guilty. You weren't wrong—I did fall in love with him. I even told him so." Juliette's brows knitted. "But he loved you so much—he wouldn't have ever done anything to hurt you.

I envied that—I envied you, and your perfect life." She was tearing up. "It was wrong of me."

Sarah was stunned. "It's all right," she said, tears coming to her eyes, too.

"He talked about you all the time," continued the younger woman.

Sarah's heart caught in her throat. "I loved him so much," she whispered.

Juliette nodded. "I know you did. He knew it, too. You should know—" Her voice dropped, almost to a whisper. "The night before he died, he told me he'd found another job for me. He said he needed to work on the marriage and couldn't work with me if I felt the way I did. It wasn't fair to you."

She burst into tears. Sarah would never have thought she could feel kinship with this woman.

"Thank you," said Sarah. "Thank you for telling me. We've made mistakes, both of us—I'm sorry, too."

They held each other in the street for a long moment, ignoring the passersby.

"I never had the courage to tell you," Juliette admitted.

"I think it's time we both moved on," Sarah said, wiping tears from her eyes.

They said their goodbyes, and to her surprise it was bitter-sweet—another part of her past that she was letting go of.

* * *

Sarah ran on.

She passed by the playground area, contenting herself with a look inside. No more visits there. Running toward the reservoir, she picked up speed, feeling her heart beat fast, the heat building in her body. It was hard and good, and she pushed herself a bit farther than she had last time, feeling the rhythm in her feet.

After a full loop, she stopped to stretch. A younger man, fit and attractive, smiled at her from across the path where he'd slowed to check her out. Sarah smiled back at him.

"Hey, Sarah!" a woman's voice called to her. She turned to see Laura running toward her. "Hey—sorry to keep you waiting," Laura said.

"I already did a loop," Sarah said. "I'm way ahead."

Laura watched as the man and Sarah nodded to each other. "Look at you!" she teased.

Sarah smiled mischievously. "You mean you can see him, too?"

Laura laughed. "Don't worry," she said, looking after the man. "He's *very* real. You got time for a full run today?"

"Maybe," Sarah said. "I'm dealing with the country house."

"That's right," Laura said, her voice growing serious. "You okay?"

"It's time." Sarah smiled sadly. "I've got a lot of great memories there—but there are a few I wouldn't mind letting go of, too."

"That's an understatement," Laura sighed. "How about the kids?"

"They understand. They're glad we're all moving on. I am feeling better about them being away at school," Sarah said.

"I'm glad," Laura agreed. "It sounds like the right thing at the right time for you."

Sarah nodded. "I think it is," she said. "You ready to go?"

They ran off together, chatting as they fell into stride.

Around the next bend, behind a tree, Sarah glimpsed a man and she felt faint. The blood drained from her face, and her running slowed down as she caught her breath. The man looked just like Lawrence. But it couldn't be, could it? She closed her eyes briefly and shook the image away. From time to time, she wondered what had happened to him and his children and if he had ever finished the novel he said he was writing. Laura was still chatting, thankfully oblivious to what was going on in Sarah's mind.

Sarah opened her eyes and quickly scanned the tree that now stood lonely in the winter wind. She would have to mention it to Dr. Benz. She kept on running, the steady pounding of her feet on the icy path bringing her back to the present. No more Thérèse. The journey ahead was still long and winding, but from now on, she would look within and live her own life. She took a deep breath and exhaled like a fire-breathing dragon, filling the cold air with smoke.

Dr. Robin's Journal Entry

It has been a few months since I arrived at the psychiatric ward. My lawyer is still getting calls from networks that want to do a movie. He believes that I have a chance at an appeal, but I'm not interested. I told him not to rush.

Being here, amongst hundreds of subjects, many who are like Sarah or worse, has been a true blessing. There is one particular patient, Katie, who reminds me of Sarah. Katie is petite and soft-spoken. She suffers from a multitude of disorders. Delusional disorder being just one of them. Katie is here for killing her husband. She has convinced herself that he never existed. I have watched her as she flirts with one of the guards, Daniel. He is handsome and seems more sensitive than the others. She is convinced he's in love with her. I have to allow her to believe that it's true. I have had two sessions with Katie. So far, she trusts me.

Sarah was just the beginning of a greater experiment.

# ACKNOWLEDGMENTS

## FROM TERESA & TULLAN

This book would not have been possible without the support, guidance, and encouragement of many people. Thank you.

We would like to express our gratitude to Jane Wesman who has guided us through this process with her ultimate wisdom and helped us find Beaufort Books. Thanks to Megan Trank, our amazing editor at Beaufort, whose brilliance and kindness made this journey a great experience. Eric Kampmann, whose wisdom and expertise was immensely helpful every step of the way, and the rest of the amazing team at Beaufort Books. Thanks to Kimberly Macleod who is not only a great friend but a great connector. Thank you to our producing partner Frank Rainone at Roman Way Productions who saw this as a film when Teresa was still at Weinstein and encouraged us to write the novel and flesh out the story. Thanks to Mike Powers, who Teresa has bounced ideas off of for years, and was one of her first readers.

FROM TERESA

I want to thank my writing partner Tullan Holmqvist who was the most perfect writing partner anyone could ever dream of.

Thanks to some of the best friends a girl could have (in alphabetical order): Antonella Acquista, Micaela Arnaboldi, Cristina Cuomo, Madeline Cuomo, Amy Porter, Lisa Sarti, and Colette Testa, who each read the story and encouraged me to keep writing and gave me input and great advice.

To my sister-in-law Marnie Goldfarb who is my soul sister and her boys who are the best nephews an aunt could have. And Rich Goldfarb for all your advice.

Thanks to my mother-in-law Adrienne Barrack for pushing the book and helping spread the word faster than any sales team could. So grateful for her help. And thank you Jerry Barrack for all your support.

Thank you to my father-in-law Fred Sorkin who was the first to buy the book when it went online and who has given me tremendous loving support. And in memory of Nancy Sorkin, even though she is no longer here, is always in our hearts and souls.

My father Rocco Launi who was a poet and storyteller. I miss him every day. And my mother Tina and brother Jian.

Most especially thanks to my husband Ian Sorkin for listening and reading and encouraging me every step of the way. You truly made it all possible with your support and love. You have been my rock. And my beautiful, smart, and funny children, Jaden and Isabella, who make life worthwhile each and every day.

FROM TULLAN
Thank you to my fabulous writing partner Teresa for a great collaboration and journey together.

Thank you to my wonderful and loving family, especially to my joyous and amazing boys Max and Leo, my extraordinary husband Giovanni, whose beautiful music and dedication are deeply inspiring, and my truly special and marvelous sisters Malin and Linda with their precious children Sebastian, Daniel, Miles, and Elsa. I am so grateful to share this journey of life with you.

Thank you to my supportive and wondrous friends and family, in particular my inspirational acting teacher Michael Howard and my writing group at the New York Society Library.

To my beloved mother Carin, who passed away during the creation of this book, profoundly loving, deep, and wise; inspiring me to compassion, generosity, joy, and, most importantly, to love. We are all one.

# BOOK CLUB QUESTIONS

## GENERAL

1. Which quotes or scenes did you like the best?

2. Did you find the ending to be satisfying and meet your expectations of the plot? Were you expecting the final twist?

3. After you finished reading, what sections of the book did you want to reread in order to spot clues you may have missed?

4. Did you come away from this book wanting to read more by these authors or in this genre?

5. Had you heard of Erotomania before? If so, in what way? Was it similar to Sarah's disorder? Have you ever felt obsessed toward a love interest?

6. In the past, famous psychologists and psychoanalysts have conducted experiments on their patients. How do feel about that?

7. There are many women in history, as well as in literary and film history, for example Medea, Shakespeare's Ophelia and Glenn Close's character in Fatal Attraction, that have been connected to madness. Are there any that you identify with? Why?

## SETTING AND THEME

1. Was the setting one that felt familiar or relatable to you? Why or why not?

2. Did you get a sense of how Sarah experienced the city she lived in—New York?

3. What was the overarching theme of the novel, and how well did the authors convey the theme? If there were multiple themes, how did they relate to each other and to the plot?

## CHARACTERS

1. Did you feel Sarah was justifiable in some of her paranoia?

2. Why do you think Sarah's son Jason is so defiant? Is he angry with Sarah or is it something else? How did Sarah relate to him?

3. Dr. Robin and Sarah's relationship is quite central to the novel. Why do you think the authors chose to include the Dr.'s notes?

4.  Lawrence is mysterious and dangerous. Why do you think Sarah agreed to be swept away? How would you describe their relationship?

5.  How does Sarah's relationship with Lawrence compare to her early relationship with Eric, before they had children?

6.  Did Dr. Robin's need for control affect Sarah in more ways than just her psyche? Why do you think she kept her office so stark and impeccable? What other therapists in literature have been similar to Dr. Robin?

7.  Why is Sarah so upset with Eric? Is it all justified? In what way has Sarah's jealousy affected her life?

8.  Sarah's grandparents protected her from her trauma. Do you feel they did a good thing, or did it enable her in a negative way? Can you think of other ways that parents or caregivers can hurt a child while thinking they are doing the right thing?

9.  Why did Sarah see herself in Thérèse Raquin? Are there any literary figures you see yourself in? If so which?

10. Is Sarah a likable character? Did your point of view about her change one you discovered the true nature of who she is?

**TULLAN HOLMQVIST** is an investigator, writer and actor and is the coauthor of the psychological thriller novel and screenplay *The Woman in the Park* with producer Teresa Sorkin. Tullan's work as a private investigator has included global fraud investigations, financial due diligence and art cases. She has a master's degree in political science from the University of Florence; literature and language degrees from universities in France and Italy; and screenwriting and acting studies at New York University, Boston University, MH and HB Studios. Originally from Sweden, Tullan lives in New York with her composer-attorney husband Giovanni and two sons.

**TERESA SORKIN** is a Television Producer with a passion for creating, writing, telling, sharing and producing great stories. She is the founder of Roman Way Productions, a production company with 32 projects in development. Teresa has produced shows and films for various networks and studios. Teresa received her degree in Marketing and Media from New York University (NYU) and Bocconi University in Milan. She was a journalist for RAI TV where she worked on entertainment and fashion hosting her own show for the network. When Teresa isn't working on the best next story, she spends time with her husband Ian and two children.